EVERYBODY'S FAVORITE BROTHER

(A Real DC Story)

BY
DAVID HARPER, SR.

Trafford
PUBLISHING® www.trafford.com
North America & international
toll-free: 844-688-6899 (USA & Canada)
fax: 812 355 4082

TABLE OF CONTENTS

11 MARQUIS OF QUEENSBURY RULES! 68

12 BALLOU HIGH SCHOOL 93

13 GEORGETOWN UPWARD BOUND 101

14 TENNIS ANYONE? 109

15 GOING AWAY TO COLLEGE 111

16 LEAVING LYNCHBURG AND COLLEGE 119

17 PRIVATE HARPER, USAR 122

18 OUR FAVORITE BROTHER 141

19 GOD SPEAKS 167

20 WHY I WROTE THIS BOOK 171

21 CONCLUSION 176

Jay & Eric smiling in Easter suits

1

"PRAYING TO GOD"

What if you were praying to God, I mean a deep, passionate cry, really "putting on the dog" as they say, on behalf of a loved one who had passed away several years ago...and God speaks to you? Audibly! You actually hear the voice of God, the voice of the Holy Spirit. Knowing what was prayed, to whom you were praying to, and the response...it has to be of God! Oftentimes, the Spirit will be a still small voice that you won't hear audibly, but you know it came from your belly or innermost being.

No one is in the house with you; you have been there alone for over an hour, it's just you and God...you alone, in your own room, at your bedside beseeching the Lord Almighty, about your beloved brother.

What did God say to me about my prayers concerning my brother? Did he respond to me about him? Did he respond to me about me? How did I interpret what I heard, what did it mean to me? What will it mean to you, the reader? Read on and I will tell you what the "Holy Spirit" said.

This is a true incident. I am not embellishing anything; this is the way that it happened. I would not write this to sell a book. I'll take this to my grave, because it is true.

2

THE EARLY DAYS

(Lickin the crumbs off of America's floor)

Let's go on a walk around the edge of my life story. It is a curvy road but one that leads to salvation! I was born and raised in Washington, D.C., the nation's capitol. I like to call it the Worlds capital, Washington, DC is THE CAPITOL OF THE WORLD!!! Growing up in DC shaped my life in a way that I find almost everything interesting, because almost everything is here. It opened my perspective in many ways. I am proud to say that I am from Washington, DC! Not braggadocios or arrogant, just glad that I learned about the world from the stand point of growing up in the Nations Capitol.

When we were young children, our parents would take us around town to give us an appreciation of the Nation's Capitol. They wanted us to learn and know what was in their city. Being both were from DC, they were young, but they knew how to make the best of things. We would often go to the Monument to see the 4th of July fireworks from the National Mall. We would get to the monument and the reflecting pool about noon and stay until the fireworks were over at night.

You know mom and dad were cool back then, especially when dad had a car. However, he would go too long without wheels of his own. Dad caught the bus to and from work for many years. We missed going places as a family. We would ride around the city by bus, usually with momma, because she took us to our appointments and stuff.

We went to the Washington Monument one day that was so fun. It was like something you would never forget in your entire lifetime! The Monument has about 898 steps and stands 555 feet, the only real skyscraper in Washington, DC! One day we took the elevator up to the last floor and stood in those windows on the top floor. Man! Looking down was so scary. It was something to see the landscape, the beautiful architecture, all of the scenery, but man, "take me down out of this window, please!"

We decided to walk back down, I mean, mom and dad decided to walk back down the stairs, as opposed to taking the elevator. We would walk and turn, walk down and turn, over and over again. I don't know how many times and then finally.....we were down to the ground floor. As we all got outside, I said the wrong thing. You know how you say something, but you meant to say something else, and you leave out a major word? That's what I did! I said, "man, that wasn't nothing!" I meant "man, those steps weren't nothing", but my dad heard me. He said "see boy, why you gonna say something stupid like that? I can't get ya'll to appreciate nothing, bla, bla, bla, bla, bla....I pouted the rest of the evening my feelings were hurt.

That's how excited I was about things, my city, my surroundings, higher learning, and sports. I mixed sports and academics into one combination. That is how I became a good and avid reader. I used to read about sports, mainly football, all of the time. Gradually I learned that sports and social life all fit together, so as I read about sports, I was learning about the society that I lived in.

I was an inquisitive person, always smelling, touching things, asking questions. Wanting to learn, analyzing things on my own. I was very touchy feely. I remember as a little boy playing with my fathers' pipe collection. He had this cool little pipe that folded up. I often would put the pipes in my mouth, mimicking him. I had a habit of smelling everything that I touched. As for touching things, mom said I liked stockings and legs as a toddler! She said I used to like to rub my hand across her stockings. Even if a visitor was in the house, I would sit beside the strange lady and rub her stocking legs with one hand, and my bottle in the other! Where did I get that from?

We were blessed with two wonderful parents. Our parents instilled in us family values, and education. My father would call us together and have family meetings, he would tell us to stick together. They gave us the best opportunity that they could give us. They had us in church, worked hard to keep food on the table and clothes on our backs.

My dad who we affectionately call "Diddy" did not have a high school diploma. However, he instilled in us the value of getting an education. He talked with us and allowed us to communicate with them, to speak our minds. He did a fine job in my book because he was raised without a father in the home, without any siblings, by his mother.

Grandma Harpy, raised her only child in the mid-thirties, a missionary and true friend to others, to this very day! She is the "sweetest lady" that my family has ever known! Raising my dad was no walk in the park, I am sure. However she persevered to give him a stable home and positive environment. She raised him right because he turned out to be a good man.

Mama was a teenager when she met my dad. At the tender age of fourteen she became pregnant with my oldest sister, Pamela. Mama did not have much of a mother figure to glean all of the important things in life from. Her mother was an alcoholic, a very attractive woman, known as "Dotty". Mama had to live with her grandparents, McKinley and Hattie Belle. I am sure they all instilled some positive values in her because she turned out "all right" as well. Mama is an all purpose kind of mother, sweet, kind, caring, stubborn, strong, and most of all loving. She and my dad made a great couple to nuture and raise their seven kids.

My Granny (Hattie Belle) had a twin sister who left the DC area and went up north perhaps. Mom said that their last name was Dreher (or something like that), but they had lost contact with her ever since.

3

UPTOWN

We grew up in a two-story row house up on Georgia Avenue. I believe I was born on a warm autumn day forty-some years ago. We might have been living on Spring Rd at the time I was born. My oldest sister was already about six and into one of the girlie social clubs. You know the one that teaches them etiquette and fancy's them up, whenever they held their social tea parties. Spring Road was a nice neighborhood with detached homes. From Spring Road we moved to Columbia Road and then to Georgia Avenue.

Then I have two older brothers and one sister after them, before me. My oldest brother and the next one were two of the best brothers to have. No kidding. They looked out for me and our siblings as best as they knew how. That in turn showed me how to look after my younger brothers in the same manner.

I remember my brothers and sisters early on, when they had to get ready for school and momma fussing at them to get their act together. I learned a lot from hearing momma fussing at them, because while she was fussing she was instructing them and me about life.

While on Georgia Avenue, Eric and JT were in the boy scouts together. Once momma sewed them two Indian suits she made from scratch. It was a great idea, but they were made of Burlap! If you know anything about Burlap you know what I'm talking about. Burlap is the material that you find most sacks made of. You might find a sack of potatoes in Burlap material. When Eric and Jay tried to take a step, they were so uncomfortable because Burlap pinches and scratches and it has a strong dusty smell. Without a nice lining you are sure to itch like crazy! They tried to put up with it, me still in diaper with bottle in hand, cannot remember how it all turned out but I remember them being very uncomfortable!

My sister Dorothy came after them, I always had in her, a sister to bounce things off of. She was instrumental in my learning because she always liked to read books, mostly the Donald Goins or "street" books, and eventually I began to read them after she told me about them. She always made them sound so interesting and I found that I could learn a lot about the streets and other elements of society, without having to go thru those ordeals myself. Those books taught me that crime and different lifestyles were not what I wanted for myself and my children.

I remember being very afraid of fire trucks because the loud sirens would interrupt my play.

You see, Georgia Avenue is a very big and fast street, especially to a toddler. One day an older boy hit me with his bicycle, I was out playing on the sidewalk and I looked up to see this bike coming right at me...all I remember is the front tire of the bike pushing me to the ground...it rolled right over me!

But hey, I was back out there everyday, oftentimes looking at the neighborhood alcoholic do her impersonation of a crossing guard. I think she would check in every Friday or Saturday and attempt to direct the traffic! Now I was only about 2 and I can still see that lady to this day! She was comical, falling down, mumbling, stuttering and saying things to the drivers.

I remember once me and my sister were in her house playing with her children, I was so afraid to have to confront that woman if she came in. I just knew she would come in the house drunk, I hardly saw her sober. But it was cool, cause I don't think she came home while we were there that day.

One day something caught fire next door, I remember the firemen storming up the stairs and throughout the house. Axes in hand, knocking holes in the walls, I wasn't sure what was going on. That scared the crap out of me too! But hey, I was just a baby, momma's baby. After all, I was getting used to Georgia Avenue, the busiest, siren-filled, street that we ever lived on!

Mom recently told me a story about the rodent infestation that we had while we lived on Georgia Avenue or Columbia Road. She said it was so bad that she had to cover up the boxes of cereal with something to prevent the rats and mice from getting in them. One day in the wee hours of the night, mom was carrying me in her arms, and as she walked down the hallway, a large rat was walking right towards her. She said, she still doesn't know what she did to this day, but somehow she scaled the walls and raised over the rat, and both of them just kept right on passing down the hallway like nothing happened.

Mom gave birth to my younger brother Sylvester, while we lived on Georgia Avenue, two years after I was born.

4

THE MOVE TO SOUTHEAST

We moved to Jasper Road, all the way in southeast, when I was about 3 years old. Jasper Road was an old house that was given to my family through the church my Great Grandma Hattie Belle attended. My father was the custodian for the Evangel Assembly church and my great grandmamma was the head of the Missionary Department's clothing campaigns.

It was a new change for all of us, my younger brother (Vest) and I spent a lot of days playing in the yard. We would run away under the porch, which was our hideout place. I discovered it when one day Vest was running away from home, so he hid under the porch. I just sort of stumbled up on him. He told me he was mad and that was his hideout. He thought we would not find him there and he was probably right.

One Christmas there, we got identical zip guns. We used to play with those zip guns in the yard. They were a lot of fun. They made this zip sound and had a light inside them that moved like a lightning bolt when the trigger was pressed. We would often play fight each other or look for the bad guys with our zip guns.

We made ice cream from the snow one winter, there on Jasper Road. It was the bomb! That was the first time that I remember tasting that kind of ice cream. We watched Batman, Dick Van Dyke and all of the cartoons, when the television was working and before our parents shows came on.

Jasper Road was on a dead end street. There was an access road with an entrance behind it that led to an army installation. I remember seeing many jeeps, and trucks with soldiers all of the time going up and down that road. The house on Jasper Road had a long hilly yard with long steps in front of it and a big back yard full of trees.

It was an old house that we had to evacuate immediately when the flying ants invaded us. They came from everywhere and raided our home! I remember coming back from church and we saw the infestation of flying ants, over every piece of furniture, and every wall. It looked like the walls and the furniture was moving because everything was covered with moving bugs. These were large ants with large wings too. I still think that they were termites!

Mark, our youngest sibling, was born on Jasper Road. I remember the evening that momma went into labor with him. I was four, almost five at the time. She kept moaning and going in and out of the bathroom. Then the paramedics came into the house and the ambulance took her to the hospital. I knew something was going on with her, but I couldn't fathom the essence of it all. Why was she in pain to give birth? I remember seeing my new little brother, and realized a little more, what all of the fuss was about.

One time I went across the street to a neighbor's house to get my sister. This neighbor had a dog, a little dog, but big to me, and it attacked me. I was scared to death, this dog barking and snapping its teeth at me...jumping up to bite me while I am running and crying for help. It seemed like a long time before someone came out to help me. I can't remember anything else after that, but I was so glad to see them come out to help me!

I remember the walk through the woods and busy streets we took to get to church. Whenever we did not have a ride we would walk, down through the woods and across Suitland Parkway, then walk up another long hill. We no longer went to Evangel Temple and had started worshipping at a nearby Catholic church, which was my father and grand ma's religion.

My older brother and sisters were all going to school by then, and I began to learn from their trials and errors. It helped me a lot that I had four examples of how to grow up, ahead of me. I learned a lot by listening to what they were going through, and from what my mom and dad said to them. That was an asset that prepared me for what was to come.

5

UNCHAINED ANIMALS IN A VALLEY OF DESPAIR

We moved to the Valley Green apartments in Greater Southeast, when I was almost five years old. Things really began to kick off. So much so, that I hope I do not forget too much of the significant things that went on there. Vietnam was in full gear, people getting drafted, going off to fight and die in a "senseless" war. The hippy revolution was in full effect, flowery, free, and freaky, with its intellectual ambiance. The March on Washington, the Black Power Revolution, the Beatles ripping the charts, while the Godfather, Ray, Areatha, Marvin Gaye, and so many others, were spinning out the hits, left and right, all of this going on central and around my hometown, Washington DC.

The projects that we moved into were decent buildings. Little did I know when we moved there, it would be the place where I would plant my roots! We lived there for about 14 years. I stayed there from four to nineteen years of age.

Back then Valley Green was like new, I mean, new to us black folks. I later worked with a lady named Mary, a white woman who said it was predominately white at first. She had actually lived in the buildings before they became Valley Green apartments, a housing project for low income families. We were termed low income families because of the proportion of income to the size of the families. Most of us had large families. The average size of a household was about six or seven people, oftentimes with one parent.

The buildings were red brick, about four stories high. They held about seven or eight family units in each building. Each unit was spacious enough for the right size family. There were nine of us, actually ten, counting my great grandmother who moved in with us also. There were five bedrooms, and two full bathrooms. Several large closets and a hallway down the back side with decent sized bedrooms. The living room was very roomy, and the kitchen was a decent size.

I remember how we had community pride back then. We often held block parties in the open courts, up the hill on Varney Street, regularly. That is until, that fool popped a gun in the air and everyone scattered!

It was so much to talk about from this era, that I don't know how much not to talk about! We had a lot of fun here. The community actually had a little league baseball team, my oldest brother Eric, was one of the players.

They would have contests for the best maintained building and outside area. The community would deliver turkeys and give away food (mostly canned goods) around the holidays. They would have people, mostly teenagers who were paid to come down to sweep and rake the grounds, and maintain the building upkeep. We kept our apartment very neat; most families in our building did also.

I remember growing up as a child playing, seeing how long we could go before momma would make us take a bath, trying to stay out late on the front porch, to play. I remember telling my friend Clyde that I hadn't taken a bath in about a week and he said he hadn't taken one in about two weeks; imagine we were actually bragging about that! It was about noon and we were already outside, just as we said that, our mothers called us, we knew what that probably meant. We were afraid of what they were about to tell us, it was "come in to take a bath!" I still don't know how they heard us to this day.

The first stunner came when I got out of the bathtub one day, wet and naked, slipper less, running down the hard-tiled hallway. I tried to stop and make a turn into the bedroom, and fell face first into the floor! Bam!!

My two front teeth were broken. I was in such pain and agony! One of my teeth was dangling in my mouth, so loose, that when Diddy used the pliers to pull it out, I did not feel a thing! I was a little snagga-toothed boy from then on. When my teeth grew back in they were bigger and I had a noticeable gap. My siblings used to tease me, calling me names like "Silly Rabbit" and "Snagga

Pus". These were names of cartoon characters with two big front teeth!

We made up nicknames for everything back then. I and my younger brothers always seemed to get the worse ones. They called one of my brothers "Ninky Noc" because he used to do a number two on himself. One of us was called "Nibble Drawers" because our drawers were always "eaten up with holes" all in them. That reminds me of all of the hand-me-downs that we used to wear. I actually looked forward to wearing some of my brother's old clothes. The shirts, the shoes, the khakis, I still thought I was cool and looked good with them on.

One day while playing in the bushes, (why was I in those bushes?), when all of a sudden, I saw a bee hive! It had bees all over it, but I did not know it. When I got too close, they got me! I experienced the most painful and annoying attack that I have ever experienced in my life! Those bees lit me up! It felt like about 20 to 30 bees had attacked me, stinging me all over my head, my face, my back. I could see them flying all around me during the attack. Needless to say I stayed away from bushes for awhile!

Thank God, I was not allergic to bee stings! Speaking of allergies, a little bit of tomato, ketchup, or grass would break me out in hives, over my back. Momma would pull out the Calamine lotion or mix up some "baking soda and water" to soothe on my skin.

I remember my first friend on Valley Avenue, was a guy named David also. He was a little older and he became my welcome to the neighborhood buddy. It was cool that we had the same name.

We rode a wagon together, down the slight hill in the parking lot next to my building, many times. And yes we fell off together too, nursing our bruises and wounds collectively, those tumbles hurt but we would get back on the wagon with excitement! Then one day David's family moved. I missed having David as a friend.

We were the second family to move into the building. Mrs. Neal and her daughter Mary Ann, were there first. We were new children for Mary Ann to play with. My sisters would spend the night with her and her mom. I remember spending times upstairs in their much smaller apartment. Mrs. Neal was a very nice lady too.

A little later a family with three girls and three boys, the Osborne's, moved downstairs, just like the Brady Bunch (although we had not seen the Brady's yet). They were a large family that became an extended family to us. Each of us had a best friend from the family and our parents were friends also. Years later, many other families and individuals came thru 961, I can't mention them all now. Most of them will be mentioned later.

Back then we played together without a lot of junk. We respected adults, and we were not the disrespectful, profanity mouthed, youngsters that are prevalent today. My great-grandmother was a strong Christian woman who taught me something very special at an early age.

I was not more than seven when I had this big blue plastic bowling ball and set of pins. That was one of the best toys that I have ever had! I was playing with the bowling set the first day that I received it, and lost the ball in the bushes. Later that day or the next, I saw my neighbor Tawanna playing with my ball. I told her that it was my ball and to give it back to me. Tawanna was about three years older than I, and her family especially her mother was not one to argue with.

I will never forget her mother, Mrs. Bea, is what we called her. She was a strong church-going woman, who had raised her children all seven or so, of them into adulthood. She might have been a widow or divorcee; often very nice, always respected by her presence. But don't get her angry at you because she would curse you out in a "New York" minute.

I had heard her argue many a day with other folks, "thiiiiis close" from a physical confrontation. She was known for saying "I will knock the blue farts out of you!" We used to have fun mimicking that statement. As the years went by and I became a teenager, I remember her walking to the bus stop, dressed up and going to church or wherever, on a regular basis.

Only one time did she say harsh words to me. Her great granddaughter, who was a lot younger than I, started physically hitting me; she was a little girl so I went to find one of her adult relatives to get her to leave me alone. I don't remember what Mrs. Bea actually said to me, but she fussed at me. I knew she did not really dislike me, so I did not take it to heart.

The things I knew she had faced in life with one son going off to Vietnam, another son who was a very hard to control juvenile delinquent, and grown daughters, grand children and great grand children, she had enough on her plate.

Mrs. Bea could be "sweet as pie," and she could be "Mrs. Bea"!

Tawanna was the baby of the family and some of her siblings were well into adulthood. Tawanna refused to give me the ball, she said "it was hers" and we carried our argument to the "Supreme Court". The Supreme Court was any adult that would preside over the case. Well this time is was Great-Grandma Hattie Belle (Granny).

We argued in front of Granny, I knew that I was right, because it was my Granny who had brought me the bowling set, in the first place! It was also very special to me because it was the only gift that I ever remember her buying for me. I said, "Granny you bought me that ball today, tell her to give it back to me!" Tawanna said, "naw, naw it is mines, I found it in the bushes. I'm not giving it back!"

Granny just looked at us and said son, "let her have it, go ahead and just give it to her." *Somehow, that moment froze in time.* I can still see Granny standing in the doorway! It was the principal of the matter, I guess, that sometimes it is best not to get worked up and fuss about the little things in life. Also it showed me a strength that although we were right, we were not defeated in losing the bowling ball. She said, "there will be other bowling balls, don't you worry". That was over 37 years ago and I remember it to this day!

6

GAMES CHILDREN PLAY

We would get together and play baseball in the driveway, about 10 of us, all of the time. I was the youngest and last one chosen. The bigger guys like Dana, Paul, Ralph, Bernard, Donnie, JT, Eric, and others would get chosen first. Clyde would be chosen next to last, and then me. They used to cheer Clyde and myself on while we were trying to get a hit. Finally I caught on and learned the art of not striking out. Clyde was hitting homeruns before I was, but I did not strike out as often.

Then it became football, we would play it everyday. Two hand touch on the concrete or black top. Sometimes we would play "Throw up Tackle" or we would have a bigger game of tackle football among ourselves or against a rival team.

Then it was basketball that soon became a year round sport. However, back then, football still ruled! We wanted to imitate all of the new NFL stars. I was a football nut. A fanatic! I knew most of the players, college and pro's. If I did not know, someone I knew would find out. That is how I became known as, "the Professor". I learned about so many other issues of sports and life just through the sport of football.

Shirelle taught us how to play "Around the World," and "Poison." Both games took a great amount of skill and savvy. In "Around the World" you had to move the big, soft, ball around the blocks in succession, as fast as you could, to keep up. If you made the ball hit the line or missed the block you were out! Whichever way the ball was to flow, it had to bounce in one of the four blocks Jack, Queen, King and Ace. The Ace controlled the game; he or she was the master. The longer you hung in the game the more that you would move up to "Ace". It was very hard to get the "Ace" out of the game because it took the most skill to get to be the "Ace" in the first place. When you did get to "Ace" it was easier to get people out, because you controlled the game. We would be lined up 14 deep to play that game for hours....slowly dwindling down to our bedtime!

The game "Poison" took more skill. You needed precision and aim to master this game. All you had to do was line up at the beginning of the game, so everybody could play together. We were oftentimes 8-10 deep playing this game. You had to throw your "can or piece of whatever" from block to block on the concrete course. It was smart to get something that would not slide very much, so cans became outdated. We painted blocks from 1 thru 12 and the poison circle. You threw your "can or object" until you missed the block. We often got into fun arguments about whether or not the can was touching the block. If it was, your turn had to stop until it came back around again. If you could hit another player's can or object they would have to start all over from the beginning. The first one up to 12 and back thru poison was the winner! Shirelle was very skillful at both of these games.

Oh, we played golf on the front of 961 also. I designed a miniature golf course, of about 15 holes, and used balls from our miniature pool table, as the golf balls. We started a golf tournament with lots of kids, and it was a hit for weeks! We boxed out there, jumped on pogo sticks, skated, rode bikes, go-carts, sleds, saucer pans, you name it! We did it all on the front of 961. As we got older it became our hang out spot to congregate before we made a move, while we listened to early Go-Go music, the Funkadelics, and all of the other hit bands of that day!

By the age of twelve I started going up to the Metropolitan #11 Police Boys Club, (MPBC) regularly. I played right tackle for an undefeated 90lb team, coached by Officer Lynch. Then I sat out the next season (because I felt that the boys were too old and too experienced for me at 105lbs, I was only about 85lbs) and played on a 110lb team coached by Officer Huskins, that following season. We were 5-3 and had to deal with a season that ended in adversity. Some of the other teams in the league had to forfeit their games because they had ineligible players. The following year I played on a team that was 9-1, coached again by Officer Lynch, and again we were champions!

Both of those coaches helped me to become the man I am today! I remember Coach Lynch's quiet demeanor, and his steady, calculated, repetitious manner in which he conducted every practice.

One day he was getting after me because the defensive lineman that I had to block kept messing up the plays. I told Officer Lynch that the kid was running all the way to the other side of the line to get away from me. Officer Lynch kept after me, I found myself mumbling back at him and he told me to leave practice. I was not sure if he meant that I could not come back and play anymore, so that was weighing on my mind as I prepared to play in the game the next day. I decided that I had too much love for the game and if Officer Lynch wanted me off the team, he would have to tell me when we lined up to pick up our uniform and equipment. I was scared and nervous but I lined up to get my equipment anyway. Officer Lynch didn't say a word about it, and I took my uniform with glee!

Officer Huskins taught us how to be tough. He taught us to not take any pity on your opponent. He used to always say "smash a knat with a sledgehammer"! I remember the time he smashed a helmet on a brick wall after we had suffered a surprising defeat. He didn't have to say a word on that bus ride because we were all quiet going back home. I ran into him as an adult at the bank, and he told me that I should consider coaching. He said I would make a good coach. That is something that I had always wanted to do anyways and I took his advice!

Mr. Sneed, my boxing coach, who I will talk about later...I can't say enough about him. His dedication and presence spoke for itself. We all highly respected him; I often observed and emulated the kind of man he was.

7

THE RIOTS

I remember the riots of 1968. Dr. Martin Luther King had just been assassinated! I remember being in about the fifth grade, it was near the end of the day. Yvette and I had just started talking, she sat across from me. She was sitting with her legs open showing me her panties. I was allowed to keep dropping my pencil on the floor so I could go under the table to retrieve it and peek at her. She was purposefully, showing me her underwear.

Then another teacher burst into the room, telling my teacher about the assassination and riots that might follow. So with that going on, we were told to gather our belongings and then walk straight home as fast as we could. You should have seen so many kids running, with scared looks all over their faces.

For a while things were cool, and then around 7:00 p.m. we started hearing about the rioting. We saw people from time to time who were looting, running with their goods in the neighborhood, to get to where they were going. Some were running from the store and some were running to the store. Then we saw big Tyrone and his boys with a shopping cart full of liquor. They were generous enough to give a bottle of liquor to others in our building. I watched my dad hide his bottle in the washing machine with some clothes on top of it. That's how it was back then; even though they were looting they still were generous to give things away.

Then about a week later, a mob of teenagers and young adults began looking for white people, who were driving in the community. This was back when all the people, black and white, were writing words like "black power" or "soul brother" all over their cars and windows. If the mob saw you were white but you had something like "soul power" written on your car windows, they would leave you alone. But if you didn't, they would attack you that day. They harassed people by throwing rocks at their cars. They even tried to get some of them out of their cars and attack them physically. I felt really sorry, excited, and afraid all at the same time.

This went on for awhile, until the police and National Guard showed up. At first the mob ignored the police. The police did not have enough manpower. The mob was about 60-75 people deep. They had sticks, rocks, brooms, hammers almost anything you can think of.

The National Guard or riot force stepped in and took control of the situation. We were looking from our four front apartment windows, three stories up, and about 50 – 70 yards from the scene. The police told the crowd a couple of times to disperse and go back to their homes. The crowd did not budge. Finally the guardsman donned their protective masks and gear. They assembled into formation, I heard the leader call out commands and I saw them move in unison, then they kneeled on one knee and fired towards the crowd! Everyone scattered!

Next thing you know the crowd was breaking up like crazy! People running everywhere, screaming, hollering, crying, and running anywhere they could, to escape the tear gas. I am sure some of them thought the police had shot bullets at them. This was exciting and funny all at the same time!

We were still up in the windows, each one of us commenting about the unfolding events. Just like commentators at a sporting event. All of a sudden we could no longer look out the window because the tear gas was coming through our window screens. We started coughing, gagging and choking until finally my sister Pam screamed, "shut all of the windows, you're letting the tear gas in!"

I had never known before how it felt to be really gagging, and coughing like that. It took awhile for us to clear the house out. We all had to put something over our nose and mouths until the gas subsided. Momma and Diddy were not home at the time. Diddy was probably working at his second job and momma was probably at night school.

Being a young kid at the time, I was scared whenever people died. The memory of their death would haunt me when I went to bed. I would think that they might show up in my room, or be under the bed. So I was very afraid to fall asleep before my younger brothers, and have to go to the bedroom first. The three of us, Mark, Vest and myself, slept in the same room and we would each cry whenever we were made to go to bed first. I thought about people like MLK, his assassination, Abraham Lincoln and Robert and John Kennedy. I would see their faces in my mind and it kept me scared.

Whenever I knew someone was assassinated it gave me this spooky aura about death. I will never forget, going to Ford's Theater in Washington, DC, the place where Abe Lincoln was shot in the balcony. Then going across the street to the house and see the bed where he actually died in. That was the worst part! Man oh man; I could not stop thinking about that stuff for years. Every time I went to bed I would think about Abe lying in that bed, about to die. I would pull the cover over my head and make a little hole for my eyes and nose. That is the only way I could get comfort. I would be so relieved whenever I heard one of my younger brothers getting woke up and sent to bed. I believe that I prayed many times for that to happen!

Diddy would say David, don't sit there and go to sleep. Many times he would tell me that and I would say, "I'm not sleep". Then I would just lay there and fall asleep. One time he took the little hose off of the washing machine and spanked my butt with it. I woke up screaming and crying. I remember momma saying, "now James, don't hit that boy like that"! I still could not control falling asleep very well after the spanking, I'm not much of night person.

8

BEFORE SCHOOL STARTED
AND KINDERGARTEN

I could not wait to go to kindergarten! I wanted to go to school so bad with my brothers and sisters. Despite having a slight speech problem, or speech dyslexia, I was a eager learner. Momma said that I loved for her to read me stories. I would even bring her the funny papers at a very young age for her to read to me, sometimes twice a day! I would sit intently while she read. Sometimes I would get in a chair or stool and read to myself even though I was only about 3 years old.

When Granny's nurse would come to the house to give granny her insulin shot, she would marvel at me because of my desire to learn to read at such a young age. She noticed the questions that I asked, and how well I sat and listened to the stories. She would ask my mother if she could read to me. She was a young white lady and she really took to me. I guess I had it going on then, and didn't even know it! LOL

My speech dyslexia was not severe. Momma noticed that I could not say all of my words correctly. She said it sounded like I was saying the opposite of what I was trying to say. She thought I was using the "f" sound for the "p" sound and the "p" for the "s" or "f". Whenever I said "fire" it sounded like "pire", "food" sounded like "sood". She was not good with phonics enough to know how to correct it. So she found help for me. I had to go to this school once a week and take speech therapy. They taught my mom and my sister how to teach me the correct sounds using special cards. I also remember the auditory sound lessons that I took. This was just before I started kindergarten, all of four years old.

I could not wait to go to school! When I got to kindergarten, I was a whiz. I was already used to the classroom environment because of my speech lessons. I remember being the leader of that classroom. I was the first one with the answers, first one in line, or first one following the correct procedures. My favorite books were, "The 3 Billy Goats Gruff" and "The Little Train that Could." I remember being fascinated with the new and different books that my teacher had in the classroom.

Ms. Moultrie my kindergarten teacher loved me. She was very impressed with me. She told momma that she wanted to talk to the principal about skipping me into the first grade. She said that I did not belong in the kindergarten any more and I should not wait until first grade begins the following year. She was permitted to have me tested, to see if I could skip into the first grade. I passed the test and after just two weeks of kindergarten, I was in the first grade!

9

GRADE SCHOOL

Boy, this was a different classroom environment all together. From the get go, I did not really like this new teacher. Ms. Holland was unorganized, and much sterner than Ms. Moultrie. There were more students in that classroom and all of them seemed a lot smarter than I was. Needless to say, I started off kind of rough. My first report card was all D's in every subject, from Speech to Behavior!

When it was time for lunch, she could never find my meal ticket. She would search all over that class room, in her file cabinets, her desk. My brothers would be waiting for me to escort me to the lunchroom and they were held up from their lunches as well.

After a while, I began to get to know some of the other kids and we began to do things for fun. Like look under the desks at the girls' panties, they were letting us do it. I even remember one of them moving her panties to the side. I can't believe now that we were doing that way back then. We did not really know what we were looking at. I began to talk a lot and get into trouble along with the other kids. My report card got better for a while, and then it went back down again.

The second grade was much better. I believe that Mrs. Bennett was my teacher. She was very sweet and pleasant. Even pleasant to look at, she was fair-skinned and had long hair. I began to really gain an interest in school there. My favorite time was P.E. and story book reading time.

The third grade brought me my firmest teacher to date. Mrs. Atkins was very strict! She had a serious reputation for being a disciplinarian. You did not mess with Mrs. Atkins. I could always get the scoop from one of my four older siblings because they went to the same school and knew about all of the teachers. What I remember from Mrs. Atkins class is the many times that we got disciplined by her. You did not want to get caught talking, playing, or not doing your work because she would have you come to her desk. There she would paddle your little hands with a ruler or point stick. Then she would feel sorry for us, give us a hug, and tell us how she did not like disciplining us. She had my respect, let me tell you! I was a good student, but I liked to talk and interact with the other students. So my mouth got me in trouble some. But not like some of the other kids. Some of them were really badd! They were the ones that were always being called to her desk.

One day in the first grade, we were lined up

in a hallway stairwell. I was apparently talking to one of my peers and the teacher came to scold me. She hit me with an open hand, a little smack across the face. My head hit the wall from the impact. I remember the sound that it made and the little bump forming on my head. I got so mad that I walked away from her and out the door. I told her I was going home to tell my momma! I walked all the way home by myself, past the woods and across the field, mad as can be! I let my mother know what had happened and she went to the school to have words with the teacher. I always had a temper but I would not use it unless I had to.

Once while walking to school our neighbor Donny, who was my oldest brothers' age, kept picking on me. He kept teasing me about something, I think he was calling me "silly rabbit" or something because my two permanent teach grew back in very large, with a big gap between them. This was a result of my bad fall onto the floor after I got out of the bathtub. I got mad at him and my older brothers would not stop him, so I took matters into my own hands.

I bent down to find a little rock to hit him with. Instead, I picked up a little shard of bottle glass, by mistake. I always walked behind the group because I was the youngest and smallest one, I couldn't keep up. I decided against throwing the rock because I might miss and hit someone else or I might hit him in the head. So I ran up to Donny and took the shard of glass across the back of his jacket.

Now this was a "cool" jacket he was wearing. It was a soft beige tweed jacket. Next thing I knew,

I had put this long slash across the back of that jacket! Much like what Zorro would have done, only I did not make the complete "Z". Everybody was like, "ahhhh! I'm gonna tell your momma. You gon get in troubbbbblllllle!" I was ashamed at what I had done. It was an accident! I didn't really want to rip his coat; I only wanted to hit him with a little rock.

Now I knew I had to answer to that incident. I was only about six at the time and later that evening momma made me go downstairs and apologize to Donny's mother. I was scared to apologize to Mrs. Alice even though she was really sweet person. I would not budge to knock on their door. I kept practicing what to say, attempting to knock but holding back. Mom sent Eric to see what I was doing. He knocked on the door and he talked me into going in there. We went in there together. I said, "Mrs. Alice I am sorry for cutting Donnie's jacket." I really was. She could see I was about to break out in tears. She just said "its alright, I've got a needle and thread". "I think it will turn out okay when I sew it up". Boy was I relieved!

I would get teary eyed at the drop of a hat almost. My feelings were hurt very easily. But don't make me really mad because I would go off! Stomping and hollering. Poking my lips out. I would throw tantrum after tantrum on my mother. I did not do that around my father too often, because he would lite me up with the belt. But boy, I had a temper. I was King Tantrum!

Mom tells a story that one day a guest on the Mike Douglas show (this was one of our favorite shows) talked about how to deal with children's tantrums. One suggestion she gave was to throw a little cold water on the child as they were falling out, all over the floor. Well it worked! Momma said that one day I went into a tantrum and she doused me with a little water! She said "all I could do was stop, shake the water off my head, and stare in bewilderment." I wasn't ready for that one.

In Mrs. Atkins' class I remember her lining us up 4, 5, or 6 at a time to get the stick on the hand. She kept her class in line; however she still had to deal with some real behavior problems from my other classmates. Those would usually be sent to Mr. Jones the PE teacher who used a thick paddle with holes in it. The holes were to make it easier to swing the paddle and to suck to your skin or clothing when it hit home. I only went to Mr. Jones for that, once!

It was in her class that she read us the Mary McLeod Bethune book. It really opened my eyes to things going on, that I did not know about, like racism, discrimination and the KKK. I realized how good we had it, and that many others went through sufferings that we could not imagine. I began to appreciate the privileges that their efforts provided for us. Oh yeah, the KKK was another one that I did not want to think about at bedtime. I got caught up in putting myself in the shoes of kids who saw their homes burned down, the crosses burned, and their fathers hung, by the masked men in the white robes, on the horses.

The worse thing that happened to me was the day my friend Janet did a bad thing to me. We were in Ms. Bennett's second grade class.

I liked Ms. Bennett so, so much. Janet was one the quietest, smartest and cutest girls in the class. We sat next to each other and our birthdays were on the same day. That day we were really enjoying each other, having a good chit chat while working. I also sat next to big Larry Worthington, who sat on the other side. I stood up from my chair talking to Larry and just as I was about to sit down, I saw Janet's hand in my chair with a pencil in it, sticking right up to my bottom.

It was too late! My weight came down on that pencil and it stuck right into my buttocks. I felt the puncture and the pencil break halfway. I just stood up, looked at Janet, and walked straight out of the classroom down to the nurse or principal's office. I met my teacher in the hallway, who took me to the nurse's office, right after she asked me what had happened, and briefly scolding Janet.

The nurse and the other faculty were in amazement about my walking with a pencil stuck into my leg (actually it was right below the buttock). She had me to lie on the table while she called my momma and got permission to give me a tetanus shot.

When my sister Dorothy found out about it, she vowed that she would get Janet back. I kind of wanted to tell her to not bother Janet, because I still liked Janet. I felt sorry for her. But, she got her anyway; I think she punched her for poking her little brother.

The fourth grade was a lot of changing classes, teachers, and substitutes. My fourth grade class was off the hook! I believe Ms. Felder was my teacher part of the year. Ms. Felder's class was almost uncontrollable. One day we had this substitute teacher who had us for about a week. One of the students kept commenting about how little she was, I will never forget the remark she gave him. She said "I'm a little piece of leather, but I'm well put together". We did not know quite what she meant so she elaborated that even though she was little, she could still kick some ass! Not to mess with her. We heard that!

The fourth grade, Mrs. Hagan's class had one too many bad boys in it. I had to learn how to deal with bullies who were quite larger than I. They pushed me until I broke on the biggest one. I stood up to him until it was resolved. About five years later this same guy came to our apartment looking for my brother; this guy was so high, everyone said he was "lunchin". That was a term for going crazy, or so high that you were always doing crazy stuff.

The most excitement I remember from her class was about Tyrone. He was the most rambunctious student that we had. He would run in and out of other class rooms hollering, to the top of his lungs, openly defying the teachers, disrupting the classes without provocation. That is until his mother showed up unannounced.

Tyrone was doing his thing in the room; his mother was standing right at the door looking through the window next to the door frame. Some of us began notice this strange woman looking into the room, all of us except Tyrone, who was steady acting up!

We were all asking, whose mother is that? Is

that your mother? "That is so and so's mother." Finally Tyrone looked and he went, "that's my mother"! His momma came in the classroom with a belt in her hand and whipped the slop out of that boy! I mean he was hollering, crying, and trying to run from her, but she was too much for him.

I am sure most of the room was amazed that there was someone who was big enough to control Tyrone! We were shocked to see him crying like a baby. She did such a good job on Tyrone that day, because when it was over we did not have the same Tyrone anymore. I don't think he disrupted the school another day for the rest of the year!

My fifth grade year was really interesting. Mr. Street was our teacher. He had a good reputation of being one of the best teachers. All of the students liked him. He was very nice, a young man in his twenties. Janice my former girlfriend was the teachers pet the year before. Mr. Street was Caucasian, in a school with only one or two white students. Our classroom was detached from the main school in an annex outside by the field. We had lots of fun in that class.

Mr. Street was a good teacher that earned our respect because he wanted us to learn and allowed us room to grow up. He let us practice a play that one of the more gifted students had written. It was a gangster play and Lafayette had written this play as if he had studied at Columbia University!

Lafayette was different from the other boys. He was not athletic at all. He was more of a nerd than anything else. This guy could not even throw a rock far. He wrote stories, poems, and plays and there was no equal, nowhere in sight! I would sit there and watch him write. We rehearsed our lines over and over, day after day, went through dress rehearsal and everything with this particular play.

However, just before the performance, the school did not allow us to put it on because the content was of a violent nature. Mr. Street would take us outside on Friday afternoons to play softball or kickball. That was great! I remember he also let us box each other with boxing gloves that I had brought to school. I boxed Donald and did a good job on him, much to my surprise!

Once Mr. Street, wrote a note home to my parents because I was caught copying off of another students paper. I remember my mom lecturing me because of the note. When she told Diddy, he put me across his knee in the bathroom and gave me a couple of licks. That note really helped me to become more independent with my school work.

He also would take 4 or 5 students to his home on the weekends. We would spend the night with he and his wife. She was very nice also. They did not have any children at the time. He had this little sports car, a convertible; it was so fun to ride in it. All of the kids would say that was one of the highlights of the weekend. They took us near the National airport onto this big field, while airplanes flew very low over our head. So low, that the noise and the size of the planes made us cover our ears and bury our head to the ground. It was such an awesome feeling. We had so much fun on the field that day. Thanks

Mr. Street, you inspired me want to do my best, to impress you with my learning and interest in what you taught us.

Now the six grade year, I was beginning to get crushes on different girls. I saw this one girl at recess, playing jump rope. Her name was Renee W. She was the prettiest girl that I had ever laid eyes on. You know the kind of pretty that only you can pick out. The kind that is just right, exactly what you would want. I made such a fuss about her to my friends and found out her name. But I was too scared to meet her.

One afternoon when school was over my friends and her friends addressed my little crush on Renee. Someone said "David, there goes Renee over there, go over and talk to her." I tried to brush off the demand but it continued. The next thing I knew more and more people were getting involved in it. They formed a crowd around us as if we were about to fight, with us standing face to face.

"Now David, what are you going to say?" "Say something David, don't just stand there", I stood there mesmerized, captivated by her beauty, afraid to say "hi", can I have a chance with you?" If I said anything, I just said "hi". I was hoping she would take the lead and say something like "I heard that you like me". But she didn't make it that easy. Everyone went, "ahhh, he ain't gonna say nothing, he is scared!" I felt like a buffoon that evening and for a long, long time after that.

It's funny that when I did pursue another girl a little later, Natalie's sister, who was just as captivating as Renee, she shunned me. I was hurt, but later I surmised it was because she was young and I was a little too aggressive when I approached her.

I wasn't really afraid of girls then, I was just used to them taking the lead. My first girlfriend was Janice. She was Donnie's younger sister; however she was about 2 ½ years older than I. I remember when we were 5 and 7; Donnie married us both, together. We had this mock wedding under the awning around the back of our building, just the three of us. Donnie had us say these wedding vows and pronounced us man and wife. Donnie being only 9 at the time was pretty good at it too!

This was the same Donnie who's jacket I had ripped (or was about to rip) some time later. He and I were really good friends after that. Often times we spent time alone pitching and catching a baseball together. I used to like to practice different pitches and he would be my back catcher, tutoring me as best as he could. I even picked up a library book that taught me how to really throw the pitches correctly. I remember that I once threw this curve ball that actually seemed to go straight, then go left, as if sideways, in a split second. We both saw it and were amazed!

Donnie turned out to be a great athlete in my book. He was blessed with speed, easily the fastest boy in our whole elementary school.

He went on to run track all of his teenage life. Traveling and sharing all of his stories with me. I used to always prod him to tell me as much as he could about his track meets, when or where he would travel. I wasn't jealous either, I was glad for him.

With all of that speed I wished that he would run track and play football in college, but he went into the Marines instead. Donnie's entire family, except for the baby sister, were extremely fast runners. They were all blessed with track speed. I often wished that I had been blessed with track speed to go along with my determination to become the athlete that I wanted to be.

The rest of the sixth grade contained a few other stories that I would like to share with you. One was the time we held elections for class officers. We all had to present these election speeches. I was running for the Office of Vice President. My buddy, David Guest, was running for President. I will never forget his speech. First of all he put some time into preparing his speech because he was more passionate and expressive than any of the others. He was the last one to take the podium.

He started out by chanting, "vote for me, and I will set you free!", "vote for me, and I'll set you free!" He wasn't shy or embarrassed, he was actually very confident! He promised us everything from an extended lunch break, to school dances every week! I thought he was being kind of silly, but nonetheless I was very impressed by his speech and method.

I was so impressed, but I kept mocking him afterwards as we went outside to lunch. We were all mimicking him. I was just doing it a little more than the others. He took exception to it and we got into a brief shoving match. It was very hard to fight one of my best friends. Finally we cooled off and made up.

There was another incident when I put David to sleep. I thought that I had killed him. Donnie had put me and JT to sleep the day before. You know how kids are, once they learn something cool they have to try it themselves. When Donnie put me to sleep my brother and I were in his room. He attempted to do my brother and it worked. I could not believe it, so I had him to do me. (I won't attempt to say how we did it because it was dangerous, we just didn't know that.) When he let me go, I fell to the floor. It seemed like I was dreaming, I thought I was falling for a long time, all I could see was tall, tall trees, as I was falling through. A little later I awoke to JT and Donnie slapping and yelling at me to wake up. It was amazing!

The next day at school I told David and my buddies that it had happened to me. They could not believe me and that I had to do it to one of them. David volunteered. We were standing right outside the cafeteria; just as I put him to sleep, I laid him down. I was shaking him and hitting him a little, to wake him up. That's when the Vice Principal saw us. He was coming over to us, so I got the guys to help me drag David away from him.

I began to slap him harder, and harder, to wake up. Shaking him, saying, "wake up, wake up!" (I must say I began to enjoy slapping him, just kidding). I was just about to get really scared that I had killed him, when he began to mutter words. He woke up finally, not knowing what had happened to him. He could not believe that I had put him to sleep! But we all convinced him that he was out like a light!

A couple of days later, Kevin put his brother Keith to sleep. I was against him doing it and wished I had not told him, but he did not listen. Instead of laying Keith down, he slipped and dropped on the hard concrete sidewalk. Keith busted his chin wide open. We were all in shock and knew that someone was going to get in trouble. All of his brothers got punished for that incident; they were punished from going to the boys club for a whole week.

Mr. Street and Mrs. Tipton, my sixth grade teacher, were two of my favorite teachers. Mrs. Tipton just had this way about her. She was very down to earth. Kevin who later became my best friend was equally as fond of her, I would find out later. Once we walked to her apartment to say "hi" to her, on our way to the boys club.

She dealt with us in manner that we felt was fair and comfortable. I just remember wanting to be like a teachers pet, going out of my way to please her. I could sense the passion and hard work that she put into being a teacher.

One time I had this stack of football cards and she asked me to bring them to her. She was looking at the cards and something made me say, "Ah, Mrs. Tipton, you just want to look at them men, don't you?" Mrs. Tipton said, "I don't need to look at them men like that, I have a husband at home."

Another time I played a practical joke on her. We had gotten this fake syringe, that had a needle on it that retracted when you pressed on it...it was a big syringe but it looked real and the needle looked like it was really going into your arm. While we were preparing to take a scholastic test, I sat there with the syringe as if I was shooting dope or medicine in my arm. Mrs. Tipton, sort of screamed at me in horror, I started laughing, and told her that it was fake.

Once she had to deal with me when I wrote this scathing attack against some of my classmates. We had all got into trouble in gym class, so she made us write about the reasons we got in trouble and what the punishment should be. I went off in my writing, putting the blame on certain kids, and she shared some of it with the class. It made me feel embarrassed, but I could then see my error. She stayed and talked with me during recess and I felt better about it. I learned from that experience.

Grade school was a very exciting part of my life. I still remember graduation day. That was such a big day for me. I had four others that had graduated before me. I was anxious for my day to come. We would always get a gift from Grandma Hoppy and from our parents. I asked my grandma for a watch. She bought me my first one which I really liked owning. My parents bought me the weight set that I had asked for. I wanted to get big muscles because I wanted to play in the NFL!

On graduation day it was our turn to wear the white shirts, blue ties and blue slacks. I remember the time I gave my mother, as we shopped for those clothes. It was the shoes that took the most time. I was adamant about getting some stacked-heel shoes, although they were on their way out of style by then.

Our graduation class rehearsed our skits and class songs over and over again. We sang "To be Young Gifted and Black". I still can remember some of the lyrics. I was excited to leave my old school and take on the challenges of junior high and a different school environment.

Elementary school had many other special moments, like the time we put on a square dance at the school PTA. We had on costumes and practiced to perfection! We drew a lot of applause. The other performances we did with Ms. Manigault, such as "Paint me a Picture", the play gangs and play fights we had at recess time, led by Lil Ronnie and Hawkeye. Hawkeye became a basketball star at N.C. State University and played two seasons in the NBA.`

The most disturbing thing that happened to me in grade school was the day that Big Romie brought in a used dope needle. He and his friends met me and Roynell coming out of the bathroom. I was at the door and I heard Romie say to Roynell, hold still while I put this needle to your arm. I don't know what got into me but I yelled, "Roynell, NO!, let's get out of here!" I could hear Roynell saying, "get off of me Romie" and then Roynell came out of the bathroom behind me.

From then on, Romie would threaten me with the "dope needle". I was sent into his classroom one day to pass a note to his teacher. When I was standing at her desk, Romie whispered, David, I got that dope needle; he leaned back in his chair, as if to show me that he had something in his desk. I was working on the school newspaper one evening after school, as the artist. I was glad that, that day I did not have to worry about seeing Romie on the way home, because I figured that he was already gone for the day. Then I heard his voice in the hallway and I cringed with fear that he might discover I was still in the building.

Romie was a lot bigger than I was. He was built like a man in the sixth grade. This guy was so big than when he went to high school in the tenth grade he became the starting nose tackle for the football team. That was no easy feat by a long shot! A day or so before all of the dope needle stuff happened, Romie and some of my friends were cool because we stopped by his apartment at recess and he took us into the basement to show us the "dope" needles that he said his brothers and their friends used to shoot up with. We saw the dirty syringes lying over the basement floor. I was so glad when he finally stopped terrorizing me with that business!

10

JOHNSON JUNIOR HIGH SCHOOL

Let me start out by saying that I am glad I made it out of Junior High School alright! Our junior high school was bad! It was off da hook! Not unlike many others in the District of Columbia. Johnson Jr. High school was tucked right in the heart of one of the worst projects in all of Southeast at the time.

The Garfield projects had gangs of bad dudes and girls who were always looking for trouble. Those brick dwellings were not apartments; they were more like connected houses. Not row houses or town houses like you see today. They were more like two homes joined together to form a small building. They had rats running through there, the size of cats! Thank God, I did not live there because their rodent problem was much worse than any project that I had ever walked thru. Every day we would see dead rats and mice on our way to and from school. Some of the rats were the size of kittens!

The closest encounters I remember with rats was the time our tub pipes had a leak. The repairman opened up the tile around the faucet and left it exposed. When I woke up first that morning, I heard some scratching coming from the bathroom. As I got near the tub, there was this huge rat trying to scramble out of the tub. It had come down through that open tile! Knowing that it could not get out, it was only trying to get out of the back of the tub, I ran the hot water on it and drowned it. Then I picked it up by its tail with pliers and flushed it down the toilet.

The other time happened well after I came home from the Army Reserves. I had my box spring and mattress on the floor. I began to notice something whenever I came in the room, but I could not put my hand on it. One day I knew for sure that I saw something run from under my bed. It moved so fast that it was a blur. I thought I was imagining something. I picked up the mattress and box spring and viola' there were three pink little baby mice. The mother had just had babies and was living under my box spring! I swept up the little mice and disposed of them. I don't know what happened to the mother mouse. However I think it lived nearby in the large adjacent hallway closet.

Johnson Jr. High was known for its fights. Gang fights with different communities. Garfield, Parkland and Valley Green were always beefing. Johnsons' reputation preceding me was worse, because the school had just opened and that was a first for several communities to interact at school. Three of my older siblings knew about more of the territory wars, because they saw them first hand. Johnson had mellowed out by the time I got there with the help of Principal Elder in his second tour.

Mr. Elder, the principal at the time was hardcore and old school! He had as much of a reputation than any community represented at that school. He was known for walking down the halls and people would hear him saying "What are you doing in the halls, I'll give you 30 days" (suspension) if I catch you! All of the people playing hooky from class would run from him. People said he would crack the stick in a moments notice. I only saw him do it once! I don't care how bad you were, you would flee whenever you saw Mr. Elder coming if you were not doing what you belonged.

Mr. Elder was not there my first year. However when he came back, I got to see the man I heard so much talk about. Once we were in Social Studies class and he heard us making too much noise. When he came into the room you could hear a pin drop! After he got finished lecturing us, he turned to walk away, when this girl yelled something like "shut up Elder". Mr. Elder turned around and asked "who said that?"

No one said a word. He began to say "whoever said it better come forward now, or else I'm gonna come back there and pull them out of the seat!" Still no one said a word. I did not even know who had said it. I was so scared of this man that I was beginning to wonder if it was I, who had said it. I was terrified that he might snatch me up out of the chair! Mr. Elder walked down the isle, right down my isle, stopped, and pulled this girl nicknamed "Poochie" right out of her seat! You could hear the sighs of relief from the whole classroom. But we didn't know what he would do next.

Mr. Elder was a man in his early fifties, grayish hair, about six feet three and over two hundred pounds. He dragged "Poochie" up to the front of the classroom. He hit her so hard with that stick pointer, that we all whinced for her.

I liked Poochie because she lived right upstairs from us. I had known her and her family for years. She wasn't known for saying anything like that or getting in trouble either. I don't know if she said it, and I still don't know how he knew, who had actually said something. Unfortunately, she paid the price that time. She was so hurt and embarrassed. I felt really bad for her.

Their brother Rick was one of my closest friends. He used to kill me with trying to walk and talk "so cool." He was my boy though! They have a nephew that went on to be an NBA player for many years, much later.

I will never forget the time that Ms. Douglas, our Social Studies teacher told me that I had made a "philibuster". The class was into this deep debate, where we were all trying to give the right answer to one of her topics. After we all had several attempts, I gave this long winded explanation to answer the question. Thinking that I had this really cool answer, that I had it all figured out, she yelled, "philibuster!" We were like, "what in the world, does that mean," laughing and stuff! I was a little embarrassed because she yelled that at me, but it was funny too!

Then there was Karen L, she was an eighth grade classmate. She started coming on to me in class, big time! Openly, in front of everybody, hugging me, kissing me, and saying all kinds of stuff like, how much she loved and wanted me. I was kind of bashful at first then I took a liking to it. One day she took it to the next class period which was Art and the teacher Mrs. Baker, took the class to an assembly in the auditorium. Karen and I snuck away from the class to mess around. Karen was all talk after all, I found out she wasn't that serious.

Mrs. Baker was one of the most interesting teachers I have ever had. She had my older siblings, so when I came through she knew me. She took to my brother JT and was surprised that I was his brother. She used to tell us these stories that I remember to this day. She talked about her experiences where people would threaten her with "voodoo spells" in college. She would tell us it was all "mind over matter". She would say if you did not believe or be afraid of the stuff, then it would not harm you. Basically, if you didn't mind, then it didn't matter! She talked to us about her Karate experiences and other stuff.

She was a small, attractive lady that really knew how to draw, a great art teacher! She inspired me to develop my drawing and taught us many techniques like how to shade. I went on to draw four busts, of some of my favorite people, they were, Richard Pryor, Muhammad Ali, Lola Folana and Pat Fischer. These were some really nice drawings, complete with different levels of shades and tones, right on my bedroom wall!

Family and friends would often stop by and comment on how good they were while I was drawing on my bedroom wall. They could not believe that I could draw so well. This inspired me to do even more. I later drew a life-size picture of the Schlitz Malt Liquor Bull. My wall was already blue, the same color of the can. We used to drink "the bull" and "ole English 800" all of the time back then. Now I wish I had used my money more constructively!

One day I thought, hey all I have to do is get my pencil and draw the bull, darken it in, and it will look just like the can! It came out really good, and it was no way near, as difficult as I imagined it would be, it was so large too.

One day one of my brother's friends named Calvin, and my older brothers were in the room smoking weed and Calvin asked, "who drew that"? They said David, my little brother. He could not believe it. I guess he thought they were pulling his leg.

One day when Mrs. Baker was out, we had a substitute teacher. These two boys who we considered were "rubber gangsters" came into our room. They were messing with the girls and subsequently they started picking fights with the guys. One of the girls, Janet Barber, told them that Hank, who was my best friend, could box. One of the guys wanted to box Hank, so he kept asking Hank, and Hank kept refusing. I guessed that soon they would say that I boxed also and he would taunt me too, so for some reason I got prepared to accept the challenge.

This guy was a little larger than Hank and

me, and I was kind of thinking, what have I gotten myself into? We slapped boxed right in the middle of the classroom, with all of the students and teacher looking on! We were going for it, as we used to say. I realized that I had enough skills to handle this dude. I was quicker and more polished than he was. We started to bleed and nick each other up. He was looking worse than I was. I know I got the best of him but I could not wait for it to be over with!

All the while we are slap boxing I'm thinking, "now all the guys can see that I can fight", and "I got to keep it up, I'm not scared of him no more". The class got really into it and they were cheering for me because this dude was a trouble maker. After the fight the dude left embarrassed, and I walked down to the water fountain with a couple of classmates. They helped to nurse my whelps and scratches. All the time they were telling me how good I fought the dude, and that I won the fight.

About a month later it was the last day of school, my classmate Jerome and I, were walking down the hallway on the third floor. We were approached by the same dude and two of his friends. The dude wanted to box me again, looking to seek revenge. I was already past them when I heard Jerome say, "hey Dave, Chuck wants to box you again"! "I just shirked, acted like I didn't hear him" and walked into the stairwell, once I got out of sight, I "hauled ass" down the steps, fearing that they were coming after me! It was the last day of school so I knew that the summer would cool him off.

Oftentimes these "rubber gangsters" would

catch us on the way to school and ask us for some money. They would pat our pockets down and we would say "man, I don't have any money". Then they would let us go. We usually had put the money down into our socks beforehand, but they did not know that. [That was basically robbery. It's funny because as an adult I ran into one of those dudes, we were boarding a bus and he needed change. So he asked me in a nice way if I could spare a quarter. I gave it to him, but all the while I am thinking about those times when they used to take our money]

The guys I hung with could fight; Hank and Kevin Wages were two brothers that were already champion boxers at #11. But we chose not to fight the "rubber gangsters" it was too many of them, plus they were in their territory. Once Kevin got into a fight with one of them and had to run because another one jumped into it. Then as Kevin was walking home from school, he heard somebody yell, "there he is!" He looked back and there were about thirty people coming after him. Needless to say, he hauled ass! The moral here is, 1) you have to pick and choose your battles, 2) sometimes you have to run, to live to see another day!

A "rubber gangster" were dudes that swore they were bad, they hung in packs, wore their shirt collars up in the back or all the way around. They pimped or moved with this peculiar walk. They skipped classes regularly, smoked weed, and drank liquor, some were already juvenile delinquents who had been to reform school.

They had bad reputations and nicknames, sometimes they were known by just their first name. They had names like Wine, Smokey, Big Finger Donnie, Fuzz, Lil Man, Lil this, Lil that. [I'm just throwing out names here (in general), because these names stand out; basically to validate and substantiate the story]. They (rubber gangsters) acted hard and shot dice a lot. That is why they needed our little bit of money!

They were quite the opposite from us. We were just a group of guys that wanted to be on the honor roll, and knew sports, like the back of our hands. My brother JT had his own crew that fit right in with the rubber gangsters but many people did not know he was my brother, and I wasn't one to put it out there. Of course his crew did not bother me and my friends, he would point out to them from time to time, that I was his brother.

I remember one day, we were standing outside the Art class, and two guys, came up to us, they were asking, "which one of ya'll is JT's brother?." I said," I am." So they said come with us. I'm thinking, oh lawd, what's going on, but I knew since they knew who I was, it couldn't be that bad. They took me down the hall and around the corner, to where JT was and asked, is he your brother? JT said yeah, so one of them looked at me and asked calmly, do you want to fight? I said "naw", he said "ok" and I just walked back down the hallway. *See there was no need to fight for nothing, what was there to prove? I was getting enough action sparring in the gym everyday.*

There were lots of fights at Johnson. So many I can not even think of half of them. But one that will always stick out in my mind is the one in

French class. Darryl probably had a crush on ZoAnn, so he took to teasing her and stuff. (Back then we would always feel the girls' behinds, but rarely did we touch ZoAnn and Sherry, because they were so prim, and proper, and they didn't seem to enjoy it like the others did)

Darryl and ZoAnn broke out into a fight. I wanted to stop it right away or take ZoAnn's place, because I did not like seeing a girl fight a boy. It did not take me long to realize that ZoAnn could fight "like a dude!" She gave Darryl a run for the money! We used to say "*she gave him a way to go!*" She was throwing straight jabs and combinations that only left us wondering, how did she learn to fight like that?

ZoAnn was a pretty, quiet, straight A student, so we were amazed that she could actually fight. (Plus you had to assume that she was not from any projects, you know?) Most of us were teasing Darryl (behind his back) about how ZoAnn had kicked his butt and that he had picked the wrong fight that day.

I was mostly concerned about ZoAnn's pugilist (fighting) skills, so I asked her where, did she learn to fight like that. She said her father taught her how to box, I said no wonder! In the back of my mind I was glad it was not me who found out the hard way. That's one reason to not fight a girl, they might embarrass you! I said to myself, that when I get children I was going to teach my girls how to box too.

I had the opportunity to run into ZoAnn as an adult, while she was dating one of my softball teammates. I recalled the story of how she and Darryl were fighting; she was amazed and bashful that I remembered that story.

I ran track at Johnson mostly because my friends Roy and Clyde were on the team. Clyde, Donnie's younger brother, was a speed burner, Roy and I were average. Roy, who was half German and Black, was just a step faster than I. He was this white looking kid with woolly blondish, brown hair. He was probably the only white kid in the whole school at the time…and he wore his hair in a bush or afro!

When we "Joaned" or "played the dozens" on each other we would all try to avoid Roy because he would have everyone laughing at you. He was so funny; you did not want to play the dozens with him. People used to call him "Sunshine", he was the one with the best jokes. He fit right in with us, just like anybody else.

Once he and I were wearing ankle weights with sand in them all day long. When we got to track practice we decided to race with the ankle weights on our ankles. That was a big mistake! Running at full speed down the hallway, side by side, just like Gale Sayers and Brian Piccolo, in "Brian's Song", I heard a pop and felt an excruciating pain in my hamstring.

I immediately screeched to a halt and lay on the floor, writhing in pain! I had ruptured my hamstring. The gym teacher, Mr. Garner, came over and lifted my legs; I'm telling him that I was in so much pain. Then he told me to rest, I was a little irked because I was thinking I needed an ambulance or a ride home!

I walked home with a terrible limp, barely able to lift my leg up over a curb. It was a good thing that Robin and Roy were with me. Robin lived just one building over so she was with me the whole way. It took us well over the half hour that it usually took. If a dog had chased us, I would have been caught. I did not get any medical attention but soaked myself in hot water and Epson salt, and it healed itself in about a month.

Then we began practicing for our graduation day. I remember we learned the song "Lift Every Voice and Sing" which was the class song. James Weldon Johnson had written this song, which became the Black National Anthem. I loved singing that song because it inspired me. I still remember the verses to this day.

Graduation from Junior High School was very special. I was now a 10th grader, a high school student, one year early too!

11

MARQUIS OF QUEENSBURY RULES!

(Boxing Memories)

I was always a scrappy little kid. I remember when Jay and I used box the kids in the neighborhood. One day Tony and Keith came down the hill and boxed Jay and I, respectively. That was a lot of fun. Keith was sharp but not as tough as Clyde, Rick, and Freddie who I had to get through in our boxing tournament one summer. Jay on the other hand found a skillful and polished veteran in Tony, but after a lot of "feeling out," Jay hit Tony with a left hook and down Tony fell, seemly in slow motion!

Keith, Hank, Kevin and Tony dubbed "the Brick-laying Wages", were veteran, champion boxers at the Metropolitan Police Boys Club #11. They had a reputation of being the best fighters in their weight classes, a mile long! I did not really know them then, although they lived just fifty yards away in the next building, 3910. We used to see them walking up the street in the early afternoon and walking back by nine. They were on their way to and from the boys club where they played all kinds of sports. I began to hang with them so much that people thought I was a Wages too!

Hank and I became best friends in the seventh grade because we shared homeroom and all of our classes. This was the first time that we had the same class. Not only was Hank in there but Clyde, and Roy too! They were two of my other best buddies.

I went up to #11 to box in the gym that I had heard so much about. I remember "fat Lawrence" wanting to spar against me. I was a year older than "Lawrence" but he was a lot heavier than I. I thought I was going to get beat up. It turned out that I was way too fast for Lawrence, and when he loaded up to swing one of those heavy haymakers, I saw it coming and moved out of the way. He was not much of a match for me and I left with a big story to tell the folks. I didn't want to brag but it was hard not to tell people the story. I told Donnie and my family that I was boxing for the "boys club". That was the first of many sparring sessions at "the club".

I boxed for about 2 ½ years, over 200 rounds of sparring. I had about ten (10) fights in the ring in front of an audience. I fought with some of the best boxers in that area, of that day. I sparred with each of the Wages brothers on a daily basis in the summer months when we fought AAU fights. This was when our team dwindled down to maybe eight fighters. I would fight Keith first, then Hank, then Kevin. Keith was the youngest, but he had the best record. He was about 40 – 2. A "lefty or southpaw," that relied on counterpunching to rack up his wins. I was about one year older than Keith, and a little stronger. Keith still gave me "some go" in those sparring sessions. He was fast and with that left handed style, punches came from everywhere. I often felt that I had to fight Keith at a lighter pace than the other two because he was the little brother.

Hank was about 5 months older than I. We were the same height and size although I felt I had slightly more muscle mass. I also felt that I was tougher than Hank, mentally and physically. Hank seemed to get better and better each time that we fought. That seemed backwards, whereas I should have been the one getting better and better, since he had much more experience than I had. Hank had a career record of about 35 – 4. Hank was a tactician, cleverly plotting, a thinking man's fighter, who used raw guile, strategy, and technique to conquer his opponents.

I remember when I first went into their home with Hank, I saw all of their trophy's and medals, seeing that trophy case inspired me to get trophies and medals just like they had won. I wanted to be a champion too! We only had one trophy which Jay had earned; I couldn't wait for our home to have a lot of trophies. *I began to put so much pressure on myself about getting a trophy, I was afraid that I could die before I would earn a trophy!*

Kevin lived and ate boxing. He was the gym rat. Kevin was two years older and more muscular (though not by much) than I. He was a combination of everything a boxer could be. He was quick, powerful, sharp, a technician with the temperament to finish off his opponents. He had the "killer instinct". I learned a lot from boxing Kevin. I boxed Kevin more than anyone else, more than his brothers. I felt that I could fight him better than Hank could. With Kevin, I had to raise my game to its highest at all times, or else I would pay for it...and I used to pay for it sometimes!

Kevin and Zeke were the reasons I had to take a break from boxing. I hated to spar with them after a while. Kevin had about 50 wins with only 2 losses at the time. I am sure that most of those trophy's and medals belonged to him. Kevin was cocky and even looked like a prize fighter in the face. He had a pug nose, and this long horizontal, scar on his left cheekbone which he got from a fall or accident. I actually saw him reopen it when he fell through the trampoline that he was jumping on. That is the way that Kevin lived "fearless and reckless".

Zeke was about fifteen pounds heavier and much stronger than I was. But, he was not very polished. When the others did not show up to train because they were all punished, Zeke and I had to spar all practice. That was one long week! I could handle Zeke, but when he got mad and unleashed some of those bombs and haymakers, Mr. Sneed, our boxing trainer would yell, "Zeke, lighten up on him, lighten up, Zeke!" Zeke did not knock me down but I was getting bounced around the mat, at times, often having to curl up to block some of the onslaught of blows. Kevin on the other hand was a better match for Zeke;

I used to like seeing them go at it.

My very first fight in the ring was a real experience. There is so much anticipation before your fights, and you wanted your folks to see you. I, on the other hand, kind of knew to not tell everybody because you never know how your first fight might turn out. You would be embarrassed if you got your butt whipped in front of the crowd. It would become a part of your reputation. But I felt that if I could handle Hank and fight Kevin everyday, then I should not have any problem with people in my weight class.

After that first round I was gasping for breath! My air supply had been cut off! My throat was dryer than the Sahara desert! I could barely say "water". Mr. Sneed had the audacity to tell me to "spit it back out"! *LOL*. Before every fight I had in the ring my nerves were almost wrecked. Imagine parachuting out of an airplane for the first time and you see everyone getting their jump before your turn. That is kind of what it was like. All I could think of was different outcomes of the fight. Would he be a good fighter? What if he knocked me down? What if he knocked me out? To my credit, I did not get knocked down in any of the fights that I had, not in the gym, not in the ring! That was an accomplishment considering the caliber of fighters that we fought.

This first fight was an exhibition fight against the Lanham Boys Club. Each fight was three rounds long, one minute each. The Lanham Boys Club was a well trained club. Trained by Mr. Tuttle amongst others, they were known for having the fighting Tuttle brothers, Charlie, Freddie, and Billy. These guys were very skilled in boxing. Charlie being the youngest was coming along, and Billy went on to fight in the Olympic trials (I believe), but it was Freddie that was the best fighter to me, he was the middle brother. *This guy fought like a black dude!* That was a compliment we often attributed to him, or any white fighter who could fight. He had a certain toughness and ring savvy (style) that most white fighters didn't have.

Kevin and Hank always used to tell me that "the white boys can take a punch." They said they were not real sharp but they were tough! I did not think that white boys could fight better than black boys. That was my philosophy at first, before I met some in the ring. I thought like that because I grew up fighting guys bigger than myself and holding my own.

When we held our little tournament in our front yard it was I who won the championship, and I was the youngest one! Rick and Clyde fought in front of judges who were our peers, and they declared Rick the winner. I fought Freddie, Clyde's tough cousin, up from North Carolina for the summer. I was declared the winner of that fight and went on to beat Rick for the championship. Rick was an easier fight than Freddie's was, because Freddie and I went toe to toe; he was as tough as I was!

My first **real** fight came as a total surprise. It was in the MPBC boxing tournament, I was fighting in the 80lb weight class. Studying the nights fight card, I noticed that they had a guy that had lost his first fight, fighting again in the tournament. I was sure of that! I brought this matter to the attention of Mr. Sneed who got to the bottom of it. Sure enough, I had to fight that night in place of the other person. I was not even prepared to fight that night, not mentally. That was kind of okay because I did not have to spend a lot of energy thinking about the fight getting my nerves worked up. I ended up fighting this dude from the Fire Departments Club. He looked a year older than I was.

I don't remember much about this fight except to say I was too apprehensive at first, and then I settled down later. He was a good fighter, we went toe to toe throughout and his nose started bleeding, but he was awarded the win. I felt afterwards that I would have won had I known I was fighting the day before. I had just sparred the day before the fight, which was a big no-no, something that we did not do! Now I was out of the tournament and had to wait later in the year to fight in the "AAU Golden Gloves" tournaments.

The "Golden Gloves" were where Kevin and Hank said you met the better boxers. They were mainly white dudes, but boxers that had achieved a measure of success from their own tournaments. These tournaments were statewide. Right off the break, I could tell that the level of intensity and professionalism had stepped up ten notches! The gyms we fought in were much larger and more people attended the matches.

There were many more family and fans at ringside. The gyms were more decorated with AAU or Golden Gloves banners. Some of the boxers actually came into the ring with robes on and real boxing shoes! We even donned robes which we did not do during the MPBC tournaments because there wasn't enough for all of the fighters on the team.

I often wanted to see my family show up for the fights, but in a way it didn't really matter. They did make it to a couple of my fights. It is hard for a mother to watch her child fight.

I remember talking to my mother in the parking lot, at home. She was sitting in the car as she and her girlfriend Mrs. Alice were about to go to an Al Greene concert. I was telling her about the big AAU/Golden Gloves tournament that I was about to fight in. That's when she told me she did not like seeing me fight.

I needed twenty dollars to buy me some new "Converse All-Stars" to box in. We called them "Chuck Taylors" back in those days. Those were the shoes I boxed in. We could not afford real boxing shoes. I liked to buy the black "Chucks" to fight in because they matched our Black and Gold boxing attire. I took my twenty dollars up to this men's store on Martin Luther King Avenue, and bought my "Chuck Taylor's".

My first AAU fight was against a very tough white kid. Mr. Sneed had just added to our arsenal of punches and I was confident enough to use the one's I had developed, once I got into the fight. This kid and I were about even. I was a little discouraged after the first bell because I knew I was in for a tough match. Mr. Sneed urged me to step up the pace which I felt I had not done enough of.

In the second round, things got better for me. I began to relax and use one of the new punches, the "under and over" during that round. It was a left uppercut, immediately followed by a right overhand. The right was my dominant hand; my left was my lead hand. This punch brought raves from the crowd. While fighting you could hear the crowd, which was a way of knowing whether or not you were doing something good, or having something good done to you!

I felt I had evened up the fight going into the third round. The third round was a war, I remember getting backed up or backing up into the corner just so I could unleash my counter-punch that Mr. Sneed had taught us. It was a very "slick" move where you waited for the opponent to throw a left, you would rock back slightly turning your shoulder as if to avoid it, and follow with a hard overhand right counter. I let go two of these punches instinctively while near that corner, and I heard the crowd going wild...they had not seen that "slick" move much at all!

I felt I had won the fight, but I soon began to learn that wins, are hard to come by with some of those biased judges. (You will see what I mean by that, later.) It was a good fight; I was humble enough to admit that it could have gone either way.

#11 MPBC did not do well in that tournament... I think we all lost our first fights except maybe Kevin and Jerry. Jerry Medley was a very slick and stylist 120 lb. fighter. He fought a war against Fred Tuttle from Lanham Boys Club that day. I knew if Fred could handle Jerry, and Jerry could handle Fred, then they were good fighters! The fight lived up to its expectations. They went toe to toe for all three rounds! The crowd was standing on their feet. As slick and fast as Jerry was, Freddie was equally as sharp and tough. Jerry got the nod. We packed up into the vans and drove back to Prince George's County.

Back then when you were little, nor knew where anything was in relation to distances, every place we traveled to seemed far away. I remember we used to fight in Rockville, Maryland, which was Montgomery County, and it seemed like a trip to another state, far away.

We loved to look around the schools that we would fight our tournaments in; we used to like to look into the trophy cases and tour the facilities which made our schools look small in comparison.

Mr. Sneed entered us into two tournaments that summer. On the way to the second tournament we went by to pick up another boxing coach and his fighters. His nickname was "Ham" and he ran the "Ham AC" boxing club. His fighters were also known to be very good. Mr. "Ham" Johnson was a vivacious and gregarious man, his presence was always felt when he entered a room. He was always talking "junk" as we called it. He brought along his son, a little boy of about 3 years old. We called him "little Ham" but his real name was James. He entertained us on the bus ride to the tournament. He was already a good boxer for his young age. He showed us his moves and boxing skills, much to our delight, he was very sharp! Ham's younger son Mark later went on to become a World Boxing Champion; he is known today as "Too Sharp" Johnson.

When we got to this tournament I fought this guy, I think his name was Mike, who gave me a good fight however he was not as aggressive as I was. This is the fight that I earned my first and only knockdown in the ring. I had been hitting my opponent all day long pretty well with everything I threw, and he did not go down. Somehow I hit him with a two or three piece combination and he flew back off of his feet towards his corner. It seemed like something in the movies. It was like I hit him, and it took a minute for it to register to him that he **had** to fall down! When he did fall down, I could see his legs and feet fly off the mat, as if he was tackled by an invisible tackler! I felt so happy, like I was on top of the world, when I knocked him down. The knockdown only seemed to make him mad because I hit him harder and harder later on, but he kept coming at me with more ferocity. I could not stop him, the fight went the distance and I won the majority decision!

I was going to fight in my first championship the following day! I was so excited. I ended up fighting this short, little stocky dude. He was very compact and looked much heavier than I did, I was tall and skinny and he was short and wide. He was the champion from his area tournament and he was warming up like a champion!

Mr. Sneed informed me to box the guy, keep the jabs in his face and move away from his punches. He said that the guy could hit really hard so try my best to avoid a slugfest. Slugging was the only way that I liked to fight. I felt that if you were going to bring it to me, then I would bring it back to you. Since I had been forewarned not to do that, I took Mr. Sneed's advice.

This turned out to be the easiest fight of my career! I mean, I hit this little dude at will.

Jab, jab, jab, right hand, stick and move, stick and move! This little dude could not catch up to me. When he would swing he would telegraph it, and I would duck the blow or side step and pap, pap, pap, a left, a right, a left, back to his head! I don't think this guy hit me five good times the whole fight! I had to have hit him over fifty times that fight!

When the decision was rendered, they said, "the winner, in the red corner, from Rockville, Joe...!" I was robbed! We were devastated! Mr. Sneed was so angry, that he was fussing at the judges, as we left the ring. Some of the crowd was also voicing their opinion with a protest of boos. This was a white crowd and white judges, television cameras were there. I got robbed out of my only winning championship!

No one could change the outcome, it was done! Mr. Sneed sat in disgust in the dressing room after the fight. He said some things to me about fighting and judges, then I remember him handing me an extra "medal", a bronze one, saying something like, "here Harper, you deserve this one too". I walked home with a "silver" (second place) medal and a big "bronze" (third place) medal. All the while I was in awe that they robbed me of the championship gold medal and title!

My second year of boxing was more fun, I was still a novice, but I fought guys in the open category. That meant that the guys I was fighting had more ring experience than I had.

My second exhibition came a year later against an opponent whom I had watched fight Keith, the last time that Lanham paid us a visit.

We called this guy "the Pelican" because he had a long face, with a pelican-like chin. "The Pelican" was tough for Keith but I figured I could whip him easily. I had this kind of nonchalant, lassie faire attitude towards fighting this guy because I was very confident in myself. I was over confident, actually "cocky"! I had seen him fight Keith, and figured I would beat him easily!

The fight with "the Pelican" turned out to be much tougher than I expected! I remember the whole fight thinking; just turn it up a notch, you got to be better than he is. I would try to hit him really hard to see if he could take it, wondering all along, if I was about to knock him down with the punch. I could not stop this guy; he kept coming after me the whole fight.

This is the only fight that I believe my two older brothers saw. I remember their stern critique. "They said, you did alright, but you have to keep your eyes open!" They noticed I was closing my eyes in the flurries, "they said I would do much better if I could see what I was trying to hit". I told them that I would just blank out, which was a bad habit from my days of fighting them. I remembered their advice and worked hard to correct it. I won the exhibition, if it had been a real fight, but I also learned a lesson about underestimating an opponent!

My next fight in the MPBC tournament was against Paul Gudger. Paul was another seasoned fighter who was from a reputed boxing family, out of #4 MPBC in Southwest D.C. Hank and Keith had fought Paul before and they gave me a scouting report. That stuff never really worked because by the time of the fight, the fighter had developed into a better or different fighter. I was still nervous before the fight, but I was not in awe of Paul because I felt if Hank and Keith could beat him, so could I! The three round bout was a very competitive one. I won the fight on points. Paul was just as tough as I expected, but I clearly won the fight, I thought.

After that fight, my next one was against... you guessed it, Hank! My best friend in the whole wide world! Two best friends pitted against one another. I felt all along that I could win the fight because we had sparred many times in the gym.

I did not really have any intentions to fight hard against him that is until Christine, an older teenager friend of Hanks said, "Ah Hank is going to beat your butt!" I was taken back by that comment and it stayed with me for days.

When the day of the fight came no one in our class knew about the fight, except Clyde. In fact we had kept it a secret from most people that we knew. Hank and I were in sixth period class, the eighth grade; the whole class was on the same exact schedule. Sometime in that class, Clyde mentioned it and I confirmed that Hank and I were boxing against each other that night. Some of our classmates started taunting us and making bets.

Hank was quiet all day and I began to notice as the day went on. When it was time to walk up to #11, Hank and his brother Tony picked me up, but Hank kept a distance ahead of us. Right as we got near the club, I asked Tony, "why was Hank walking ahead of us?" Tony said something like, maybe he is thinking about the fight. I realized then that Hank was taking the fight very seriously and I wasn't. My whole attitude about the fight was, I wanted us to fight to a draw. That sounds silly now, but I did not feel that we had to prove we could beat each other.

We were each given two of our peers to be our corner men. Mr. Sneed had a policy that whenever two of his fighters fought against each other, he would not take either corner. I had Andre Bethea and another dude in my corner. I don't remember who Hank had in his corner. The corner men were just as pumped as we were. They knew how close we were friends.

After the opening bell, I came out playing with Hank. Not punching real hard, he seemed like he wanted me for real! It became evident to me that he was serious, when he hit me with a succession of three left jabs; my head went back like a punching bag. I said "Ahh, Shucks"! "I'm gonna fight hard now!" Then the bell rang. When I got to the corner they were all over me, telling me that he had won the round. They did not have to tell me to pick it up; I already had that in my mind. I was embarrassed when I took those 3 straight jabs to the nose!

The next two rounds I felt that I won them when I went to my normal aggressive style, Hank did not hurt me or get me in trouble, after the first round. I felt I was the aggressive fighter, and had him on the defensive (the most), the rest of the fight. However, the judges saw it differently and awarded him the championship. It was a close fight. I felt like I could have won, had I not gave away that first round. It was so good to get that fight over with and be friends again. Hank's father was glad too, he congratulated us both and gave us a dollar to eat at McDonald's. Hank and I left the club and grabbed a bite to eat together. It felt like we were becoming friends all over again! Dorothy had asked Hank before the fight if we were going to remain friends afterwards.

Once this fight was over we headed back to the gym some time later to prepare for another AAU/Golden Gloves tournament. As soon as we got to the tournament we discovered that there were only two people fighting in our weight class. Hank and myself! Mr. Sneed did not want us to fight each other again so soon, and neither did we. It turned out that there was this kid who did not have anyone to fight; however, he was a little heavier than we were.

He was about five pounds heavier, which seemed more like ten pounds once we got in the ring with him. His name was Terry Buckner, he was a white kid. Terry was so thick that when he jumped up and down before the fight, you could see his chest muscles moving. You know, going up and down, how those boxers look when they pounce around before the fight. Hank and I, we were so "bony" that our little "bird chests" did not have enough muscle mass to move around. This was a sign that we were in with a much stronger fighter. To make matters worse, Terry was a "southpaw fighter"!

Hank ended up fighting Terry first. I remember the instructions that Mr. Sneed gave him because Terry was a southpaw. He told Hank to move to his left all the time to avoid getting hit by Terry's strong left hand. We also had to switch up our stance to a "southpaw" stance; this would negate

Terry's effectiveness. But that strategy was the main thing that hindered us the most.

When the bout started it became very evident from the second round on that Hank was way over his head fighting Terry. I had never seen anyone control Hank the way that Terry was handling him in the ring. He was hitting Hank so hard and so much that, Hank had little balance left. Hank had Terry in the corner and Terry picked Hank up and placed Hank in the corner. Hank looked at the ref puzzled and asked "did you see that"? Kevin was furious as he watched the fight. He wanted to fight Terry after the fight; I said "no Kevin, don't do that, you will get us all in trouble".

Kevin did not have a fight that tournament because his only opponent caught "poison ivory" and could not fight. Kevin was itching to "steal" Terry in the face once the fight was over for beating up his younger brother. Kevin was screaming out directions to Hank, we all were, loud enough for Hank to hear us, but he seemed to not hear us. Hank almost suffered his first and only "TKO", but he managed to hang in there for three rounds.

My fight was the very next day with Terry. Mr. Sneed was pulling out all of the stops. I remember watching him be very meticulous about my preparation. I on the other hand, was not scared about fighting Terry. It was a challenge to me because I had to fare better than Hank. Mr. Sneed told me to keep circling to my left and to fight out of the "southpaw stance", with a few more tidbits, just like he had instructed Hank.

I looked across the ring and saw what Hank

had described the day before. Terry was prancing, bouncing, and his chest muscles where moving up and down…this was a phenomenon to see that on a kid! The first round was interesting. I was allusive, quick, hitting Terry without getting hurt by him. I don't even remember feeling his hardest punches because I was able to "stick and move" from him for the most part. I would fight him from my normal stance, moving either way I felt like it. At times I would switch to the southpaw stance and move to my left. The bell rung and I felt like I had fared much better than Hank did and was on my way to pulling out an upset!

The second round started, things were going good for me in the first 40 seconds. I fought this round from the southpaw stance, circling to my left. This made me feel awkward, mechanical and totally out of rhythm. Terry began to connect really hard with his punches. Once I got hit by his left hand, I knew he was a heavy hitter. He hit me so hard that my mouthpiece came partially out of my mouth. I had to avoid him by running away from him, with my mouthpiece hanging out my mouth! That gave me time to put my mouthpiece back in my mouth. Terry then caught me with punch after punch. He knocked my headgear around on my head, and I was looking out of the ear piece for a second! I had to quickly adjust my headgear while I ran away to find myself. I had to hold on to him constantly to avoid getting knocked out!

Once he hit me so hard, I was knocked out on my feet! It became pitch black in the gym and I could see a "Fourth of July" fireworks display! No kidding, I actually saw the most colorful stars and fireworks that I had ever seen in real life! I remember thinking, "wow, you actually see stars and they are colorful!" Just like when we were kids and my dad used to take the family down to the Washington Monument to see the "4th of July" fireworks display. They were the prettiest fireworks I could ever see in my lifetime. Terry hit me again and I began to regain my vision. It was like he turned the lights off, and turned them back on again! I held on to him as much as I could to regain my legs and my senses.

All along, I knew that I was stinking up the joint, and building my strategy for what to do next. I could either give up and get knocked out or fight even harder. I choose to fight harder! I didn't want to get knocked down or knocked out. As the bell rung, I walked to my corner with one resolve; that was, *to fight him my way from now on!* No matter how Mr. Sneed would tell me to fight, I was not going to listen. Mr. Sneed was sure enough excited, trying to pull me together, concerned, and telling me to do certain things. I remember him saying something like, "you're way behind, you have to pull out all of the stops!" He wanted me to stay in the southpaw stance and circle left...I hated the circle left part. I stopped short of telling him that I was going to deploy my own strategy from now on! I drank the water and got my strength.

When the final bell rung, I stepped to Terry with that ghetto mentality, I had to rely on. I felt like "come on white boy, I'm about to put it on ya!" I turned to my stance, left hand in front, feet dancing ready to go either way, and pop, pop, pop, move, pop pop boom! I was throwing lefts and rights and moving and sticking! I knew that if he wasn't hitting me and I was hitting him, then I was doing something right! Terry and I went at it the whole final round without him getting me in trouble again. I may have taken one or two of his hard punches but I was better than that fighter that he saw in the second round. We could hear the people in the audience going nuts! We could see them standing up, coming to the ring apron! I really did not know that it was that great of a fight to them, but it was. I was glad to redeem myself, and win the last round.

Terry was awarded the decision, but I gained the moral victory. As we walked from the ring, I could see the people staring at me, clapping, and smiling, shouting things at me which I really could not understand everything. At least three different white men would walk up to us and say "sonny you did really well in there", or "I like the way you came back on that kid", "you did not give up", "he was much bigger than you were and you fought him like a champ". I got as many accolades after the fight as Terry did.

This turned out to be my last fight. We were set to fight in the Washington, DC boxing tournament, the "Mayor's Athletic Tournament". I had my sights set on it before Terry's fight but I bailed out before we started training for it. Kevin and I were talking about leaving boxing for a short period of time. I just wanted a break but it turned out to be permanent. I stayed away from the sport and Kevin got back into the gym a couple of days later. He really didn't tell me he was going back; I felt I would have continued if I knew that he was still boxing. I regret that I did not fight in that tournament. I would have had months to decide if I wanted to continue boxing after that tournament.

I also regret that I never talked my decision over with Mr. Sneed before I left the sport. This was a decision that haunted me as I saw other fighters like Sugar Ray Leonard make it to the big stage. Kevin fought another five years in bigger tournaments and the Air Force. Flip Johnson who also grew up with us, and started boxing at #11 after I left, won the New York Golden Gloves in his weight division. That was one of the titles that we all had coveted.

The first trophy that I ever should have won would have been a golfing trophy. The Mayor's Athletic guy had come to McGogney Elementary recreation to give a golf tournament. The workers for the Mayor's Athletic tournaments would come around and have us compete in football, baseball, basketball and golf. He would give a tee shirt to all of the participants and a trophy to the winner of certain events.

We had the golf event and we used golf clubs and this little pad with a hole at the end of it. We had to hit the ball down the pad into the hole. It was about twelve of us competing against each other. We were all lousy at first. Then I became one of the first ones to make it. After more attempts it came down to about three of us. I hit the ball in the hole more than all of the others. In fact, it came down to me and this older girl. She hit the ball at the hole and missed. I hit the ball into the hole; they gave her a second go. I should have been awarded the trophy right then, but the coordinator said "ah, let's give her another chance because she is a girl". After some hesitation, since everyone insisted she get another chance I gave in. She hit the ball and made it in. I hit the ball and missed it. They declared her the winner and she took my trophy home. I wanted so badly to take that trophy home, even though it was a golf trophy. It would have been my first trophy ever! I was only about eight years old and that would have been a big accomplishment!

Do you know what it is like losing something that was rightfully yours? Not to mention losing to a girl, heck she was older than I was! I felt likc I had lost another bowling ball in the grass, to Tawanna.

Golf just wasn't what little project boys did everyday. Heck we hardly ever played golf. We would play two-hand touch football on the concrete. Or occasionally a game of tackle on the grass, those were the days. The good ole days, when the McGogney Elementary School, we called it the "Rec" would throw a Friday night dance. We jammed to Earth Wind and Fire, The Jimmy Castor Bunch, Rare Earth, Kool and the Gang, Mandrill, Herbie Hancock, Archie Bell and thc Drells, among others. People would be in the dance from 10th place, Trenton, Congress Heights, Trenton Park, the high-rise, Valley Green, Wahler Place, Ninth Street, almost anywhere. We were enjoying ourselves, there would be a crowd or two over there, the crap game outside, and people just mingling, having a good time. This is way before people got bad, bad, really bad, and would talk about shooting.

Easter family picture (Mom taking picture)
Vest, Mark, David (Me)—front
Eric, Dorothy, Jay, Pam—back
Diddy (Dad) with outstretched arms

David (Me), Pam
and Vest, (Pam)
modeling one of
the first garments
that she made

Renee and Mark standing beside our building
—View of Oxon Run from the Valley facing
towards McGogney Elementary (background)

Mom and Dad
(early 1970's)
Happy and sharing
a drink

Boot Camp,
Fort Dix, NJ,
U.S Army, 1979

Jay, Pam, Jonathan & Eric
Chillin on a Saturday afternoon

Graduation day, Kennedy Center, 1978
Diddy (Dad) and Me posing afterwards

12

BALLOU HIGH SCHOOL

Frank W. Ballou Sr. High was the school that became my new home for three more years. It was a welcome change right off the bat, for two reasons. One, we no longer had to walk the eight miles or so thru hostile territory just to get to Jr. High school. Two, we only had to walk about three miles and did not pass thru any neighborhoods that were hostile. We didn't have to short cut through any cemeteries or woods either.

We were basically closer to our own turf so there was a greater sense of ease. Actually all of the Garfield and Parkland students were farther away from their home. I wonder how they all got to school back then. I am not sure if they walked or caught the bus.

Ballou was different than Johnson because those three years went by so fast. It seemed almost like a blur now. I remember dissecting a frog for the first time in 10th grade Biology. I studied Literature with two of the finest English teachers I ever had. Mrs. Boragard was a "beast" (I mean that in a good way). She kept things so interesting and allowed us to have fun while we learned.

I remember her breaking down the Beatles song, "Lucy in the Sky with Diamonds" and gaining an appreciation of the lyrics. Once I knew what the song was talking about, whether her information was correct or not, it gave the song a whole new meaning. Basically, she said the song was about an LSD trip...get it...Lucy, Sky, Diamonds? Listen or read the lyrics and see if it makes sense to you.

She had us bring in our favorite songs and let us play them. Then she dissected the lyrics of each song bringing out the true and sometimes hidden meanings. I remember Rick my homeboy, bringing in "School Boy Crush" by the Average White Band, and he lent me "The Traveling Man", I can't remember the artist. It starts like this, "Hey, I'm going away! I'm leaving today! I'm gonna start my life all over again"....!

Ms. Perotti had us read Shakespeare works, and Macbeth specifically. I did not think I was going to understand them, let alone like it. Once we got into them, she broke them down to where we could relate. She also brought them up to modern times. I fell in love with her class and loved to read the parts of the plays. The plays helped us to deal with some of the drama in our own lives.

Mr. Konschznick my Algebra teacher was one of the best teachers that I ever had because he taught Algebra so clear, I discovered that I actually liked math. Now the word problems were still a challenge, but it amazed me how easy they became once he broke them down for us and solved for the answers.

I took two years of French from Mrs. Cunningham, she could speak French very well and was a good teacher. I did not become fluid in speaking French then, but now I believe I would grasp it, with a better work ethic. Let me digress, I also had French from Ms. Francis at Johnson. The "finest" teacher (physically) in the whole school!

Mr. Davies our Physical Education/Health teacher used to have us write for ever! He would stand up at the board and write. Then he would move over to the next blackboard. After that, he would ask us if we were all finished, erase one board and write some more stuff. There was not a health definition that we did not write down! (Later, I realize that he was the schools basketball coach when they were "big contenders" with the Campbell brothers. Mr. Davies wasn't coaching anymore, when I was there.)

Being a 10th grader I wanted to play football so badly. That was a lifelong goal. However, since I was skipped early in school, I was by many standards too small to play, even the junior varsity. I played 125lbs at the boys club and I waited until my 11th grade year and tried out for the varsity team. This was right after I had left the Georgetown Upward Bound Program for the summer. I remember walking up to the football field for the first day of tryouts. I was too early because the actual practices had not started yet.

So I ran around the track a little before I went back home.

Somehow I found out about the practices and I began my journeys each day, by myself to football practice. We used to have two-a-days and there I would be, sweating, snot running down my face. My sinuses were so open that snot ran out my nose right into my mouth! I could only spit so much with a mouthpiece and helmet on. Then my back started to ache. I had some slipped disks in my lower back at least that is what I was told they might be. However, I kept on practicing with the pain, eventually the problem went away.

I was going out for the cornerback position; I don't know how I ended up there. I believe there were too many guys going out for wide receiver, so I was one of the few that they converted to cornerback. I only weighed 132lbs., 140lbs with full equipment on! I was like the proverbial joke, where they say "he doesn't weight 100lbs with rocks in his pockets!" I was small by many standards but determined. I was a good athlete even though I had poor eyesight. I never competed with corrected vision.

If you played for Ballou, you remember Coach Cut-Away; rumor had it that he had a tryout with a professional team after starring at Federal City Community College. "Cut-Away" was his nickname because he would make us do this exercise called the "Cut-Away"! You would usually be in the push up position and then he would yell, "cut-away"! We had to throw our arms out to the side and let our bellies flop to the ground. The bad part was we would do about 25-50 at a time. Once he was mad at us and he made us stand up, and when he yelled "cut-away" we had to fall to the ground on our bellies!

I later met coach as an adult, and he was a different person. He and I were at our children's school, which was a Christian school in Suitland, MD. I believe that he had become born-again, (same as me) and his demeanor was totally different. He did not act like the stern coach, he was back then. You know how when you were little, big adults seemed so much larger, but he did not seem as imposing and he had this happy look on his face that was not the usual stern look.

After about the twelfth day of two-a-days, I decided I had enough. For one thing, I had no friends to even walk home with me after practice because no one went that way. Secondly I was so tired and beat up when I got home, all I could do was lay on the sofa in agony and pain, gearing my mind up for the next day. I told my mother that I was going to quit. I did not go back the next day.

A day later, momma told me that Head Coach Hargrove had called, as soon as I heard his name, I lit up! "Yeah, what did he say?" "He wanted to know if I was coming back. He said that they had a scrimmage game in Herndon and he wanted me to go." Now that spoke volumes to me, because out of almost 90 guys, I thought that he did not notice me at all, this little 132lb kid, who was a year younger than his classmates.

I did not make the varsity, but I did play on the JV squad. We had the left over equipment and uniforms. We played about six games and then my high school football career was over. I did not want to go back out for football in my twelfth grade year. My mom and dad had split up. He was not there to share in that experience. It seemed like when he left, a little bit of my love for football left with him. I did not want to do it alone again. I did not want to go out for the team and walk alone all season again, only to get home and not have my dad there to share in my aches and pains, to motivate me to continue.

That was my first big mistake, because all of my life I had wanted to be a football player in high school, play in college, and make the pros. I had never even entered the thought in my mind, that I would **not** be a success on the football field and in the classroom, by the time that I graduated. I put my dream on the shelf, thinking that I would pick it up again later in college. I had a strong desire to pursue a college degree in Physical Education. I wish I had someone to redirect me back to my goals!

I stayed current with my academics, however; I started smoking weed and drinking beer more with the guys, but I still went to classes, and only had a half day of school in the twelfth grade. I still had strong ambitions to go to college, play football, make the pros, major in Physical Education, and become a PE teacher if I did not make it in pro football.

I also should have given baseball, cross county track and tennis a try because I was good at all of those sports, but without direction and motivation, I fell short of achieving those goals. I still regret those poor decisions to this day!

I spent a whole lot of time thinking about my parents' breakup. I had overheard the conversation and kept replaying it in my mind. I kept seeing my dad as he walked past me and out of the apartment for good. I remember sitting in my classes thinking about not seeing my brother, that was also beginning to get next to me.

In the tenth grade at Ballou, I had to spend a whole week in the hospital. It was the first time that I ever had to stay overnight in a hospital. It was a day or so after Christmas and I had been eating lots of pumpkin and sweet potato pie. I was sitting on the floor playing ping pong on one of them new Atari games with my friend Chris. We were laughing and having a great time. All of a sudden I got these sharp shooting pains in my chest. I had had a sharp pain or two before at various times in my life so I thought they would go away. But they did not this time. I tried to stop moving and breathing hard to see if they would subside. When I took a deep breath, I felt them again, ricocheting throughout my entire chest. I just sat there and told my brothers that my heart was hurting. When my parents came home I told them that I needed to go to the hospital. I actually felt that I should get in an ambulance but I was too embarrassed to be brought out on a stretcher.

I was admitted into the hospital to intensive care and that is where I spent the night in a room full of other patients. My heart seemed to not hurt anymore and I was petrified that I might have another spell of shooting pains.

When I woke up, there were about 6 more days of tests, observations, hospital food, and lying up in the bed waiting for visitors. I was so glad that I was released to go back home.

My doctor, Dr. Kim, a cardiologist, told my mom that I had a small angina. I was diagnosed with having a heart murmur. I had known a boy named Randy who wanted to play football with us at the boys club, but his parents would not let him because they said he had a hole in his heart, or a heart murmur. I had felt sorry for Randy because I would have cried if I were denied the chance to play football. Dr. Kim told my mom that I could still play sports but that I had to learn to stop or slow down whenever I became fatigued. He basically told me to take breaks more often and not go as long as I used to go. I was out of school for a whole week, this also was a first. It felt so strange going back to school, but I couldn't wait to be back with my classmates.

13

GEORGETOWN UPWARD BOUND

I spent a large portion of my high school years in the Upward Bound Program at the Georgetown University, GUUP. In the winter months we had to go to classes on Saturday mornings and then about noon we received our $5 stipends and rode the buses back home.

Once school was out for the summer we packed up our bags and lived on the campus throughout the week. On Fridays we went home and Sunday evenings we went back to campus. That was a really big event in my life. It was so fun to leave home and be amongst old and new friends on a university campus. We used to throw parties almost every night.

We had a basketball team that competed against the other Upward Bound programs, like Howard, and Trinity. Once we took a trip down to Georgia and played a game against the Upward Bound program from Atlanta. That was a neat trip, visiting some of the historical black colleges. Staying in a hotel room was real cool because that was probably the first time I had ever stayed in a hotel, which was probably the same for many of us.

I had a crush on a girl named Joan (the only fake name in this entire book), at the time, and also kept my eyes on Bridgette too. I was a year younger than my class because I had been skipped. I was reserved and quite, when it came to girls. I was cool once I felt accepted, but that took awhile. I remember it took me weeks to ask Joan if I could have a chance. I was afraid to be rejected. She said "maybe" or something, but ever since then we became boy friend and girl friend. I remember the relief when I finally popped the question! Later that night we took a picture together with my arm around her. I kept that picture for a long time, because Joan was exactly what I wanted!

My first date with her was when I rode the bus up to their home. I put on my new school clothes which I had bought with my summer job money. It was a tan shirt and blue slacks. I was so sharp! I had an umbrella with me and I walked about two miles, through some woods and past some apartments and houses to get on the bus. One bus took me over to Joan's housing complex which was about a 15 minute bus ride away.

She lived in Woodland which was another housing complex with a very bad reputation of having rough dudes in it also. Actually, Woodland Terrace was considered the baddest of the bad in Southeast, especially when it came to football. Their football team was said to have been undefeated over a span of many years!

I got off the bus and walked down the street looking for her apartment. I found it eventually and she took me inside. I met her sister as Joan and I sat on the couch, then we started kissing, before I left to go back home. We would talk on the phone often once we were out of the Upward Bound Program.

I remember lying on the couch talking to her for hours, waiting for her call. Falling in and out of a deep sleep, I was so in love, momma asked me if I had someone pregnant, because I slept so much.

She and Antoinette, who hung out with Fred and myself on campus, almost got caught smoking weed in the park. It was so funny to see how everything played out; Fred was more experienced in that kind of stuff. Thank God, the Georgetown University officer was cool too, because he did not mess with us too much.

Fred was one of the smoothest dudes I ever hung with. He was not like me but we clicked right away. He was not into sports as much. He had that "rubber gangster" characteristic, but he was not imposing. He was more of a slickster. A guy that shot craps, dressed really nice with the shirt and short sets, slick tennis shoes, and cool old man summer hats. He could blend with the ordinary guys and the guys that hung on the street corners.

He used to talk real, real slow, never sounding like he was talking fast. This is probably why we clicked really well because I said what I had to say fast enough and that gave me time to listen to what he would say really slow.

Fred was so comical it was ridicules. I got caught smoking weed with him twice. First in the park and the other time it was in his dorm room in New South. We had tried to mask the smell as best we could but we opened the room one time too many, and Mr. Von Cooke got a whiff of it as he passed by. He caught us red-handed and reported us to Ms. Rena the program's director. I was so ashamed that it had happened. I couldn't face standing in front of her but we had to deal with the consequences.

Another time Joan caught the bus over to our apartment and we had time to sneak away to do the "nasty". I had no experience but I did not want to tell her that. I tried to play along like I was experienced but I had a couple of questions that I should have asked my older brothers about, to straighten out my anxiety before that moment came. I was so infatuated with her that I hoped we could overlook any mistakes. It's funny I was reading all types of things for adults like the "The Sensuous Man", but none of them really touched on the very basic things that I wanted to know, because they assumed that everybody reading that book already knew those answers!

Things did not go right for me, I had just woke up from a deep slumber when she arrived, and I was still not fully awake. I knew that since she had this large scar on her thigh, I did not want to look at her and ask what happened or something, so I barely looked at her body. Then I could not get ready, if you know what I mean? My mind was not fully ready and I was nervous. Again it was my first time going that far!

We did some things, kissing, caressing, but as soon as we put our clothes back on I became ready! What a bummer! The little window we had before my mom would come home was closed! I had long anticipated getting me a piece! I felt she was a little upset but I was more upset because I wanted to finally be able to say, "I got some!" The lesson here kids is, *save yourself for your marriage*! Young boys don't be afraid that you will die before you ever get a piece, chances are that won't happen!

We drifted apart after that, I thought she became distant on campus. I walked up to her one evening and tried to ask what was wrong. She told me through an older friend, Ronald, that "I did not want it". I told him to tell her that "I did want it". She told him to tell me "well you must have not needed it then". I learned then that there was a big difference between *wanting and needing something*!

Janice was my first girlfriend, but Joan was really my first love because we were teenagers. She was very "special" to me. I was really attracted to Joan. It broke my heart the way we broke up, it really did.

We had some exciting times at Georgetown. I saw some things there that I never expected to see, racism, wantonness, drugs you name it. Once this classmate named Howard, a big muscular teenager who played tight end for Anacostia, went on a jog. While jogging he came down with this allergy, I heard him running into the dorm hollering, and crying, he was saying "I'm old, what's wrong with me, what happened to my face! I looked at his face and he had aged

80 years!

His cheeks were sagging; he looked like an elderly man. He said somebody get me some help! All of the adults were still in the cafeteria about two miles away. I took off running after them not planning to stop until I saw one of them. I was running like I was in a marathon past people, jumping over hedges, running thru and around people, taking short cuts, until I ran into Mr. Moriarty and Mr. Von Cook. I told them frantically to hurry up and see about Howard, something was wrong with him. I thought Howard was about to die or something. Thank God he turned out to be okay.

We shot a lot of ball inside and outside of McDonough gym. I remember the time that Coach Thompson was having his basketball camp. He had his young guys huddled around him at one end of the court. Since I wore eyeglasses, but did not have them on when I played basketball, I could not quite make out that he was in the group. I started shooting the basketball into the basket at the other end of the court. All of a sudden in a loud, demanding voice, Coach Thompson hollered, "boy if you don't get off of my court", I went oh, my fault, and walked off embarrassed, that I didn't notice that 6'–11" tall coach towering over the boys.

We did some mischievous things, things that normal boys do and I always hated doing them. I was not one to do mischievous things if it meant bothering someone else or risking getting into trouble. I felt it was not worth it.

One night we came across this Trinidadian (I'm not sure now who they were) party in one of the great halls. We were allowed to go in, and little by little we felt accepted and comfortable. We had a great time partying with a culture and dancing to music that we knew absolutely nothing about.

While we were in Upward Bound at Georgetown, the second year, we put on this stage production of West Side Story. We had this lady director who had some stage experience and was said to have come from New York. She was very stern, demanding, and did not take no junk off of us teenagers. She got our respect really quick, everyone of us.

In a little time, she fashioned every piece of our play, from the parts, to the wardrobe, the music and the sound. I had a large part but a very small speaking part. The only thing I said in the whole play was "por favor". My buddy Gary was the main character and I was one of his sidekicks. West Side Story turned out to be a "hit" with the crowd. We put on one performance for all of our family and invited guests. We actually performed it in the little theater on the Georgetown campus. That was a really special day. I admired the director for sticking to the script and making performers out of us.

Upon leaving Upward Bound, they threw this dynamite dance in the Hall of Nations building. I got my man Clyde from the neighborhood to go. We bought a six pack of Colt 45, 16oz and drank three apiece. We caught the bus there and got a ride back. We got lit up (stoned) in the bathroom; Clyde had to vomit in the stool. We weren't the only ones in there getting "lit". Everybody was sharing and making conversation.

The one flight of stairs, about 20 steps, leading up to the dancehall, looked like 100 steps when we came out of the bathroom. We danced and partied all night to "Fly like and Eagle", the Commodores, Isley Brothers, Play that Funky Music, and all of the other tunes that were popular.

I went to Upward Bound for two years, however for my last summer I decided not to go back. That was a big mistake! Staying home was no fun. Too much idle time, drugs, waning ambitions, babies to take care of, those dreadful soap operas. No job, no money.

I finally found a job near the end of summer. I was working up Northwest at the Crispus Attucks recreation center, cleaning communities. We would go into alley ways and fields clean them up and landscape it. That was really cool. It gave me something to do, I got to meet people and learn my way around the city.

This was actually about my fifth job. My first summer job, I was a tutor and taught two little girls while working at the Van Ness Elementary school. My second summer job, I worked at the Boys club doing all sorts of labor, from landscaping to janitorial. I also worked in the EPA Library as a clerk while in the twelfth grade.

14

TENNIS ANYONE

Tennis is a fun sport for all people to play. It is called the "romantic" sport. That is why "zero" is called "love" in tennis! I learned to play tennis from Dr. "Jake" Jacobs before I started high school. He was legendary in Washington, DC tennis circles. He was at Hillcrest Heights recreation center, before he came to Congress Heights as the tennis coach. Some people called him "Doc" and others called him "Jake".

I remember first trying to play at Hillcrest against guys that were very experienced. We didn't even belong on the same court, we were that bad. After two weeks of repetitive practice, tennis became much easier, but it seemed like I would never grasp that game in the beginning.

"Jake" taught me how to grip the racquet correctly, how to step when stroking the ball. He had this calm and teachable demeanor about him. Probably already in his 60's, he had everyone's respect and was well liked. He said he was a fullback on the Ohio State football team back in the old days, when there were only two blacks on the team.

He also coached Arthur Ashe, when Mr. Ashe was a teenager. Dr. Jacobs took us to the professional tennis tournament when it came to the Carter Baron Park one summer. He wanted us to see Arthur Ashe, his protégé.

Arthur did not play that day but when his practice was over, Dr. Jacobs called Arthur Ashe over to us. As Mr. Ashe was crossing the court towards Dr. Jacobs, the crowd of people in the stands (other teams) rushed down and crowded Mr. Ashe. Dr. Jacobs told us to sit still. We never got the chance for him to come and speak to us as planned.

I was a decent tennis player. I played every one of my matches close enough to win. I won one official match and came in second place in one tournament. As a young man, I played in this tournament down at Turkey Thicket Elementary school. I just barely lost my match, but I had played great. I didn't go back the following day to pick up my trophy.

I should have played on the high school tennis team. I was very gung ho to play at first but for some reason, after the first tennis meeting at the school, I changed my mind. I never went back for any practices and I knew I could have been one of the productive players on the team. There again, I followed bad judgment and the wrong crowd which prevented me from being the sportsman, I had always envisioned myself to be.

15

GOING AWAY TO COLLEGE

When I left Ballou I was not really ready for life because I did not have enough direction. My parents had separated and my dad and I did not stay in constant contact, like we used to. I had wanted all of my life to go to college and major in Physical Education. I wanted so badly to play on its football team to earn a college scholarship.

Since I had average scores on the SAT, only the $1500 grant that everyone else had, and applied too late, I was turned down from attending the one school at the top of my wish list, Morgan State University. I heard over the radio one night about this organization that would help get high school students off to college. I caught the bus down to this place on Good Hope Road to find out about going to college. They got me in touch with this school in Lynchburg, Virginia, called the Virginia College, formerly the

Virginia Seminary.

It was an old school run by this Baptist church organization. I remember the Greyhound bus ride after my mom and her friend took me to the bus station. It was kind of lonely, knowing I was really leaving home for awhile. I had been off to camps, two weeks at a time, twice before, but this trip was for a much longer stint. The Greyhound bus was not full, there were only about ten of us. I wondered if we were all going to Lynchburg.

I remember there was this one guy, another teenager on the bus. He too had boarded the bus in DC. He was black also, maybe a year older and twice as built as I was. His name was Edward. I later learned that he had played football at Fairmont Heights, and was a very good defensive end.

We rode the bus some six hours before we got to the bus station in Lynchburg, VA. I did not know that Virginia was so big! Lynchburg was so far away! By that time I found out that Edward was going to the same school as me. So I felt kind of better, knowing that I had someone there from the DC area there too.

I saw another student there while we were processing into the school. His name was Tyrone. Tyrone was from Philadelphia. I thought it was cool that his mother had driven down from "Philly" to get him acquainted. I wished that I had gotten that kind of treatment. Then I thought it was especially cool that his older brother had driven down with his other things. I knew it was special to have an older brother to do something like that for you.

While Edward and I shared the same bathroom, Tyrone and I became good friends. The dorm rooms where like small motels with a bathroom in the middle of two rooms. You could go into my room on one side of the building and walk through the bathroom that joined Edwards' room then straight out the other side of the building. That is the side that Tyrone's room was on.

Edward and I did not hang together but I knew he was on my side. He was only planning to be there for a little while until he could get to a bigger school and play football. Later on a guy named, Butch became his roommate, and they hit it off right away. They used to crank their music loud all of the time. Usually I heard LTD singing "Concentrate on You"; I think Butch was in love with that song. Butch was about four years or more older than myself so he was like a big brother to Ed and I. They used to have girls over; they were quite the players back then.

Tyrone was a talented basketball player from Roman Catholic High School. Tyrone had a girlfriend and a baby back at home. He could play some basketball! He told me that he was in the same backcourt with a guy, who went on to star at the University of Maryland. Tyrone did not play much basketball with us outside because of his knees, but I could tell that he was good by the way he dribbled and dunked the ball with ease; he only played games when we were in the gym.

He had a little refrigerator in his room which he kept stocked with Miller beers. I would chill out in his room and we would watch TV and smoke. I learned a lot from Tyrone and the guys, because all of the guys were a year older, more experienced and from different cities. It was he who first turned me on to one of my favorite songs "You Send Me" way before it hit the DC area.

We used to walk down through the big park on our way to the stores which were considered the mall. I could not believe how big Lexington Park was! It was the biggest park that I had ever seen. I always had a love for parks, places to chill outdoors. I'm an outdoors person by far.

I also had some friends there from places like Roanoke, and other parts of Virginia. They were so different than I was, more southern bred, with different accents and manners. I will never forget the two brothers I used to hang with from Danville. It was Joe that I walked with to see a recruiter for the first time. He had decided that he wanted to go into the regular Army after a year of college.

The recruiter and Ken sold me on the Army and I decided to go to the Afees in Richmond, VA with Ken to process in. We had a nice time in Richmond that day. However the next day when I was getting processed, the Army guy looked at my birth date and asked me about my age. I told him I was seventeen but that I was away from home already in college. He told me that I needed to have a parent's signature to enlist. The recruiter had forgotten to ask me if I was eighteen. I went back that day kind of upset that I had not enlisted with Ken into the Army. That maybe was a blessing in disguise.

Later I met Lucinda, she became my girlfriend. She lived just a block from the college. She had a little baby girl already. We hit it off right away. She and I would walk and talk, kiss, and show me around to her friends and family. I know she really liked me and I liked her. It only lasted for about a month or two before it broke off.

The guys at Lynchburg College were cool. We became buddies easily. Each guy sort of trickled in one by one, throughout the school term. There was Joe from Detroit; he was a laid back dude, and my second best buddy. The guys from the country, Woogie, Ken, Joe, Michael, they were the first people to tell me about cable television. I did not know what HBO was, until they told me about it. I was like, "no kidding man; you mean that you see nudity in movies on television?"

Then there was Julius and Fred from NY these were two of the first people that I really heard "rap". This was in 1978 and I was amazed at how well they could "rap". Oh yeah, there was also Ray with his NY accent, and he could "rap" also. I think Ray was from NY, and all over, he had lived many places, that dude was wild and a lot of fun. He always had you laughing and thinking because he was a bright dude, kind of crazy (wild), with a lot of street stories.

After a while, a new infusion of people came to the school, some from DC like Brian, who played on my high school JV squad. His cousin Toni who became Butch's girlfriend. Michelle who liked me in high school, she was in Mrs. Boroguard's Literature class with me. She had a baby by then.

The college was poor and run down. The classrooms were in this building that had these wooden plank floors. One day in class someone lifted up the plank and there was the ground just about 3 feet below. The school was unorganized by my standards.

The lunch and dinner they served us were nothing to brag about. I did not like them much at all. The dinner was okay, but the lunch and breakfast was nasty. The sandwiches they used to give us were packed with mayonnaise. It was almost a waste going to the lunch room sometimes. Not to discredit the ladies who cooked, it was the quality of food that I did not like most. I had to get used to how the sausages, eggs and mayonnaise tasted.

I was used to fixing my breakfast every morning at home. Man, I would have like three sausages or bacon, three toasts, two or three eggs. All of the name brand stuff. I knew how to hook a breakfast up! My mom and sisters could "throw down" on a Sunday dinner. So I knew what good food tasted like!

I needed a little cash to supplement my stay out there so I took to the work study program. Mr. Murphy was supposed to be in charge of it. I said "*supposed*"! He told me and Joe to clean the little area around the school, which we did. When we went to collect our stipend, he gave us this little *BS* about not paying us because we did not do what he wanted. I was furious! This man was playin us! At the next meeting we had with the school administrator, I voiced my concerns.

The school Administrator used to meet with us about once a week (all thirty of us) at the whole school. He used to preach and lecture us about the school. My friends had started telling me things like how the head guy that ran the school had to be stealing the money because the school was run down. There were no nets on the tennis courts! The food was terrible and the school house was in bad shape. They said the President of the school drove around in his Mercedes visiting the campus once in a while.

I was sitting in that meeting boiling over at what this administrator was saying. Then I got up the nerve and spoke with passion about the poor management, the work-study coordinator that did not want to pay his students, for a fair days work. Most of the students were nodding with approval as I spoke. I felt embarrassed afterwards, but I knew in my heart that I had the guts to speak for all of the students.

I walked to the lunch room afterwards in my own thoughts, by myself, feeling a little ashamed. I sat by myself because for some reason, I felt like I could have hurt things for all of us. Ed and some of the guys took note of me and told me not to feel bad and to join them at their table. They told me they were glad that someone had spoken out and that they had wanted to do the same thing. It made me feel much better that I had not lost touch with them.

I went out for the football team at the Virginia College. It only took me a couple of weeks and a few words of wisdom from my friends that I should not play for them. I went to the practices and I saw all of these old dudes running around catching the ball and stuff. Some of them had on their work uniform pants and tee shirts. I wouldn't be surprised if some of them were in their thirties. We only had about 12 guys in the whole school and I think Brian was the only one to play. Ed and Butch did not play on the team either, even though they both could have played for most Division I schools.

There was no football field, no real uniforms (well they were crappy) and terrible equipment. There was no athletic department or facility. It had to be way below the standards of a division III school.

I don't know where the coach and the players came from. The practice was so unorganized and they were talking about playing schools like Liberty Baptist, and UDC! Were they out of their minds? I had enough sense to realize that we were not on that level to be playing schools like that!

I knew that UDC had players who could ball! Like "Yip" Chisley who was a four year starter and All-American from Ballou, when I went out for the team. He was also in my Chemistry class. Yip went on to play for the Washington Federals in the WFL...and that was just one guy that I knew! Plus Liberty Baptist had a good team. I said no way; I'm not going out there to get creamed! They got "crushed" every game, you should have seen those scores.

The closest I came to playing with them is when I rode the bus to DC with the team before they played UDC. Some of us rode on the floor of the bus and was appreciative of the ride, but I got off that bus somewhere on Capitol Hill and found my way home! I didn't even go to the game.

16

LEAVING LYNCHBURG AND COLLEGE

After about five months, I became homesick, now I wish that someone had talked me out of it. I did not have a roommate for most of that time. By the time that Raymeon became my roommate, I had already made up my mind to leave Lynchburg and return to my hometown. I think that most of us were talking about leaving but I wish that I had stayed the whole year now.

My sister Pam tried to talk me into returning when I got back home, but it fell on deaf ears. I'm glad she tried though; I only wish I had listened. By giving up on college and Georgetown Upward Bound too soon, I missed out on some valuable social and learning experiences.

Coming back home seemed to diminish my socials skills somewhat. I noticed that I was more happy and gregarious around people in school environments. At home I became more withdrawn because I often spent time alone, while my friends had made new friends and moved on to other things. Now I can see that it was meant to be. It was not all a negative. I was just looking for the right situation.

I remember the time at Georgetown it was dusk; our group of Upward Bound students was strolling down the street, next to these five story dorms. I had been walking with the group really enjoying myself and for some reason I got ahead of the crowd for some self inflection. Just ahead of me, this flower pot made of clay came bursting down on the ground.

Our director Ms. Rena was upset, and rightfully so. She went up to the people upstairs and demanded an explanation. She said that someone could have gotten killed if it had landed on their head.

The people said they were sorry; it was an accident, someone had sat inside the window sill and knocked the pot over by mistake. We thought that it might have been an intentional act of hatred and racism.

Another time I was walking alone down the street at Georgetown and someone in this car of people screamed "nigger" as they rode past. That gave me a taste of racism. Those people did not know me, I thought to myself. I knew all white people were not racist. I had met too many of them that showed a genuine interest in me as a human being. They treated us like they were no better than we were. People like Mr. Street, Mrs. Boraguard, Mr. Moriarity, Mrs. Perrotti, Ms. Cunningham, Mr. Konschnick, to name a few, taught and mentored with compassion and genuine respect.

17

PRIVATE HARPER, USAR

After leaving college I began to really miss it because there was nothing to do at home. So in May, I joined the Army Reserves. My recruiter was a bronze medallist boxer in the Olympics, Sergeant Charles Mooney. I decided to go into the Reserves because I did not really want to commit to the Army for four years.

I was sent to Fort Dix, NJ for basic training. The Army was fun and challenging from the beginning. Meeting new guys and gals who liked to drink and talk was really cool. We drank going up on the train from Maryland. Just being on a train for the first time was a blast! Carolyn, a young lady from Delaware, and I became close as we talked and drank most of the way up there.

Going to boot camp was kind of like going on a shopping spree, getting fed great food and being in reform school, sort of, at the same time. (I learned later that some guys were in the Army because a judge had given them the choice to either enlist, or go to jail.) I knew right off the bat that I had to get used to taking orders from any and everywhere.

We were ordered to do everything. Go here, line up there, run here, report there, do this, do that, fix your clothes this way, shine your shoes that way, cuff your pants this way, stand over here, stand over there, salute, attention, at ease! "Hurry up and wait" is a familiar expression in the Army, that's what they always made you do.

They took us to the barber shop and it was like you were a sheep going to be sheared. We were in a long line and when your turn came you just hopped up in the chair. You could not tell the barber to take a little off the sides or just cut a little off. No! Everybody got the same haircut basically, bald!

All you could see was hair flying everywhere, most guys had big afros or long hair. Some guys had cuddies in their filthy hair, and the barber would not even stop to clean the blades! It was strange seeing everybody go in one way (wild and disheveled usually), and come out looking completely different.

Basic training was full of challenges, orders, running, exercise, food, learning, and lots of other stuff. Some of our drill sergeants were Vietnam "ready" (veterans) and very experienced. They were pretty cool though.

I remember the time that I sent a letter, but I had accidentally addressed it to myself (don't ask me how I did that). When the mail call was called, I rarely received any letters, especially in the beginning. It was tough at times, seeing others get mail almost every day, and I rarely heard from my folks, it seemed.

One day my name was called to get a letter, I was so happy. Then Sergeant Recamper who was passing out the mail, made a comment like "look at this dummy, he addressed the letter to his own self! You will never amount to anything." I thought he was kidding, but I saw that I had made that mistake. I was in a rush to get out that letter and half noticed that I addressed the envelope wrong. He was being real mean to bust me out like that, I thought.

He called me into his office later after that to berate me some more. By the end of the cycle he was pretty cool with me. I remember being around him while he watched the Philadelphia Phillies (his favorite team) play a baseball game. He was like a different person. He was actually smiling and happy for a change!

Another time we had just finished everything for the day and all of the guys were taking showers and getting ready for bed. I had just stepped into the shower when I heard the whistles blow. That meant we had to get back outside, on the double! It turned out that as the only lady drill sergeant was walking down the hall someone whistled at her. She was a cutey but kind of masculine.

Whenever a drill sergeant walks down the hall, everyone is to stand at ease on the wall, and not say a word. So when that smart ass, whistled at her he made it hard for everyone else. First of all you are never supposed to address a drill sergeant in a disrespectful manner. I rushed out of the shower to run and put on my clothes. I was running behind because I had just got under the water, so I decided to leave on my tennis shoes, which I used for slippers, and got into formation. The drill sergeant, saw I was "out of uniform" and gave me the blues for it. I never did that again!

I was moved from one room to another room, across the hall, so I had a new group of seven bunk mates. The first room was cool; there were about 4 brothers in it. There was Harris from Ohio, and Charles from Buffalo, NY who made the room fun. Charles loved to talk and was always smiling.

The other room had some real jerks in it, well maybe just one, but I had to straighten him out. His name was Robert. He was this bulky guy from Alabama. He was outwardly racist or (shall I say) opposed to me from the beginning. He thought he was tough and acted like I was supposed to be scared of him.

One day he and I got into something about the barracks floor, right before our inspection. He offered me to go to the "hole". I let him know that if he wanted to take it to the hole, we could go there and duke it out. The hole was this small concrete staircase block. This is where they would send you if you wanted to fight somebody. He realized that I meant business so he laid off of me after that.

After growing up in the projects, I was not afraid to duke it out, if I had too. I was kind of skinnier than most guys but I did not back down from them. Some guys tried me but I let them know quickly that I was no punk.

I would help defend anyone, white or black,

that I knew would not take up for themselves. I would tell them to not show fear and fight back the best way they could. If I saw them getting the raw end I would stand up for them.

When we went out into Wrightstown (the city), I met this dude who sold me some tea or something, passed off as weed. I was furious and went looking for the dude. I ran into some "brothers" on the street and they started talking to me, trying to run some game. I was already mad, so they could see I was not acting like a chump. I asked them if they had seen the guy run past them. They seemed like they were in on it too. Then I said to one of them, "Hey you look just like the dudes brother".

My buddy Daniel, this young, small, white dude from California, told me we should just leave before we start some trouble. Finally I took his advice and left before I suffered an additional loss.

That night turned out alright because just down the street we met up with some other Army mates from our battalion. They told us that two of them had bought these hookers and had rented a room. They were laughing at this one dude who had gotten rolled by this hooker. I couldn't really laugh at him but it made me feel like I wasn't the only one that lost some money. We all went back to the room and crashed out, sleeping in full uniform where ever we were.

That next morning we were walking around the town kind of disheveled when we ran into these MP's who reprimanded us and warned us to get back to the base before our curfew. It felt good leaving Wrightstown to reenter the familiar environment of the army base.

Guys were doing stupid stuff to get in trouble. Some of them actually got kicked out of the Army. One dude used to always yell, "Choke your chicken"! Everybody would "crack up" because he would say it in front of the entire battalion. They got tired of his behavior and he was shipped out.

I was in Bravo Company, third battalion and third brigade. We were Bravo 3-3. I liked most of basic training because we ran and sang cadence all of the time. I remember when we first went on a long run many of the people were out of shape. Some of the ladies, the real fat guys, and some of the smokers did not have enough wind and endurance yet. Some of the ladies could run the whole distance in the beginning of the cycle, without being moved to the back, where they were able to walk.

By the time we were near the end of basic training all of us could run the entire way. One time we went on a 20 mile jog. We ran for almost two hours straight. Let me tell you, some of the guys breath used to stink like crap! I smelled fumes, like I had never known to come from someone's mouth. While you were running you could smell the guy's breath in front of you as they were breathing hard.

I never knew that some people's breath could stink so much. There was this one guy from Butte, his breath was the worst of all. His breath could make an onion cry! Every time you talked to the guy you would get a whiff of his breath. I remember thinking do most of the people from Montana breath stink like that?

The Army taught me how to shoot. It taught me how to take my M-16 apart and put it back together. It taught me how to clean on a regular basis, from the barracks to your boots to your rifle.

I qualified as a sharpshooter with the M-16 and the grenade. We got to shoot the Light Anti-tank Weapon (the LAW); it was the most powerful weapon that we got to fire in "Basic." It could put a hole in a tank. We got to fire the machine gun also. I thought I was Machine Gun Kelly with that thang! The instructor told us to say our name and social security number as we held the trigger back. I held that trigger so long I must have said my middle name too. He said something to me afterwards like, where you from son? I said Washington, DC he said "oh, no wonder."

Throwing the hand grenade was the only thing that freaked me out. We heard all of the stories about throwing the live grenade; that some people would drop theirs and the instructor either fell on top of the grenade or pushed you to the ground. Usually someone got injured or killed.

I was petrified for that event to come. They handed us the grenade in a canister and we had to run to a bay on their command. Once in the bay the instructor would take the grenade out of the canister for you and hand it to you. Then he would say ready, cock, pull, release!

Once it was thrown he would yell, hit the dirt! I threw my grenade and it went away, but at an angle to the right. It was much heavier than all of the "dummy" grenades that we threw, so my throw was not as far as I had liked. Boy, I was so glad when that was over, I did not know what to do. You would have thought I had graduated from college or something!

One day I was assigned to guard these old barracks beside some train tracks. They took us all out to different locations in a truck and dropped us off two at a time. Me and my fellow soldier walked and talked for two hours or so until the truck came back to pick us up. I had to go to the bathroom really bad but I decided to wait just as the truck pulled up to get us. When I got back to the room I was too tired to take a shower and go to the bathroom. *What did I do that for?*

I had this dream that I walked down the hallway into the bathroom and stood at the stall. I let go this long relieving piss that emptied my bladder. I was awakened by the soldier under my bunk, because my pee had dripped through the mattress down onto his bunk. I was lying in a bed full of pee! I thought I wanted to die! He might have thought that I was paying him back for him not wanting to see a picture of my girlfriend when I asked him, but I wasn't.

I had to get back on the bus in a stinky, wet uniform. I could hear some of the guys laughing, talking, and pointing at me. I could not wait to get back to the barracks and take those clothes off! After that I really did not hear anymore about it.

We finally went out to the woods to camp out for about 3 days. My foxhole mate was this big white guy named "Oliver". He was tall, huge, with red hair and a soft, kind face. He was a gentle giant, large enough to play tackle for the New York Giants! I was glad I had him as a foxhole mate. We came to know one another during the time we dug that foxhole and pitched our tents.

He was a better camper than I. He already had experience pitching a tent. Me, on the other hand did not know one thing about tents and camping out. He assured me that every thing would be alright. I had no problem sleeping on the ground in a sleeping bag and waking up in the morning air. As a matter of fact those nights of sleeping in the tent was some of the best sleep I ever had!

On about our third night we had to partake in the long anticipated "war games". That was when the drill sergeants would be the enemy and they would fire simulated rounds of bullets, bombs that lit up the night, popped and exploded in the air, and real tear gas. These things were not designed to hurt you unless you were unfortunate, by some freak of nature.

Let me tell you, I had never been so scared in all of my life! They had us out a long ways away from our tents, on the way back they surprised us. Once it got dark you heard the whistles of bombs then loud pops, the crackle of machine guns and M-16's. They shot bombs that lit up the woods; you really had to hide because the enemy could spot you in the light.

The drill sergeants being the enemy could find you and capture you, you did not want that to happen! After they let the tear gas go, I wanted to shit in my pants. One of the soldiers yelled "tear gas"! We had to pull out our gas masks and put them on. I had trouble putting my mask on with my eyeglasses so I took them off. I could not see well at all after that.

You wanted to run, and run fast which I did, but run where? I realized that I might fall into someone's foxhole and break a leg or something. I didn't want to run too much because I might run a long ways from where my foxhole was and never find it.

All I remember is I started whimpering, "Ma I need your help!" I had a flashback to when I was a little child. I did not know where Oliver was, all you could see was people running around frantically looking for their foxholes. Once you got to your foxhole you had cover and you could shoot from there.

After awhile of jogging, jumping, hopping around, calling for Oliver, I heard him say "over here, Private Harper, I am over here". Man, I was so happy, I wanted to kiss him! Boy, jumping in that fox hole was like "home sweet home." We acted like real brave soldiers from then on. We fired our fake rounds and threw our fake bombs at what looked like the crazy drill sergeants, who were running around scaring the crap out of everybody. At that point it really became a game, but before that it was sheer misery!

We also had to go through another night of simulated warlike maneuvers. I remember us being sectioned off into groups of about eight. We had a guide who took us around the course out in the woods. At one station you had to fire your weapons, everything was hurry, hurry! Then they took you to the place where you had to crawl under live machine gun fire! If you stood up by chance you would actually get blown away, so they warned us many times to not stand up and get hurt. You had to crawl some forty yards while you heard the machine guns blasting away from this nearby building. There is this tale of a guy that encountered a small snake in his path, and when he got to the end of the path, he was holding the snake in his mouth or hand!

Then we were rushed to the tanks and actually got to ride in a tank. Boy that was so nice! I mean the feeling I had getting into such an awesome piece of machinery. Sitting in its little space with the eight or so other people, watching how the soldiers maneuvered and guided this big, expensive piece of equipment. Wondering to myself man, it would be nice to know how to drive this thing. Then we got out and completed our course. That was some night!

Each of the drill sergeants, I found were special in a certain way. Each of them were unique in how they lead the cadence. I just loved to hear most of them lead the cadence. They really knew how to bellow out those words. Those cadences were the commands that we used to sing when we marched or jogged. For instance, "I used to drive a Cadillac, now my back pack's on my back! Sound off one, two, Sound off, three, four!" Boy, just learning and singing all of those cadences were almost worth the price of basic training by itself.

Sergeant Swanson was my favorite because he was always cool and calm. He was a Vietnam veteran, in his early thirties I presume. He would teach you in a clear, concise, basic way, which made you, feel special that he took the time to help you. The one thing I remember most about him is the day near the end of boot camp; we were on our way to the supply barracks. He had us to jog in formation.

He gave us a command to slow it down, which we barely did, so he commanded us to slow it down even more, we slowed down even more, then we were jogging faster again. He told us to slow down again, we did for a while and then we were going fast again. Then he stopped us and hollered at us, "When I say slow down, I mean slow it down, soldiers!" We were jogging so slow after that, we were practically walking. To this day when I am jogging and I get tired but want to keep going, as I slow down to a walk, I can hear Sergeant Swanson yelling "slow this got damn pace down, soldiers"!

Sergeant Recamper, I talked about earlier. He was the meanest little drill sergeant that I ever new personally. He was something right out of a movie. All the guys had to say was "Recamper" and you knew to jump. In the Army there is this expression that says, "if a drill sergeant tells you to jump, the only question to ask is how high"! Sergeant Recamper was the epitome of that expression. He was ornery from the first time we saw his face. He reminded me of the drill sergeant in Gomer Pyle, MD. I mean he was just as tenacious as that drill sergeant. Always in someone's face, and as short as he was he was usually looking up to them. He was not a built dude either but he let it be know that he was a mean son of a gun!

Even in basic training we found times to drink and get high. Oftentimes they would take us down to the canteen and we could buy beer. That is where I first started drinking Michelob's, those brown 16 oz. bottles. They were so good! One Sunday evening, about our fifth week, they lined us up into formation and we marched down to the canteen. We had no idea that the drill sergeants were going to allow us to drink until we could not walk anymore.

I had about 3 or 4 beers, one Michelob after another. Just about everybody smoked cigarettes, I didn't really, but every now and then I would bum a cigarette to see what it was like. I never liked them. We all started off slow, light chatter and socializing. Before you knew it we were all loud, talking and laughing. Those people really knew how to drink, I thought I could drink you under the table but they had me beat! I was not the drunkest one in the bunch.

We lined up in formation to go back to the barracks, but it was so hilarious! People had forgotten how to sing the cadences, no one had their balance so people was popping out all over the place, stepping on heals and toes. Private Harper from California who often led cadence was about as bent as any of us. He was about 25 years old already; he was hilarious when he got drunk. He could not keep himself in order, let alone us. When we got back to the barracks Private Harper vomited right in front of the drill sergeants' door! The drill sergeants, some of them did not go with us, knew we were drunk as skunks. They stood there laughing at us. We all had hangovers the next day but it was a lot of fun.

One of the funniest days of all was the day

one of the soldiers got a package from home. He was from Kentucky, the "blue-grass state". Someone had sent him a small package of some weed! He took me and a couple of other buddies along to open his package. All I could think of was the nerve of these people sending that stuff onto an Army base (that was more common than I knew). We went out to this big field, right out in the open. We smoked those joints and got lit up! Now I know why they call Kentucky the "blue-grass state"!

When we were done we went over to the commissary and had a lunch that was second to none. The commissary was a kind of elegant hall that captured my attention, just as well as the food itself. Then we went over to look at some items. I ended up purchasing this silver plated blue stone ring that had the U.S. Army insignia on it. It was really special having that ring, until I lost it a couple of years later.

After graduation from boot camp we were all sent on coach buses to our next destination elsewhere in the United States. This bus ride was the bomb! Usually when we rode a bus in boot camp we were packed into these funny looking buses so tight that we were physically right on top of the four people next to you. It was something like when 10 people pack themselves into a Volkswagen, only we were standing up. We used to call them the "cattle buses" because of how they looked. Our next training was called AIT (Advanced Individual Training) and my AIT would be in Fort Lee, VA.

I was assigned to Quartermaster school. My MOS was cook. I believe it was the 98th Papa

Company. Everything about this place was sort of surreal. From the structure of the buildings with its huge rooms to the open concourses that went from end to end, which we called "the bays". This place seemed just like the boy's village I had seen in the movies. It was way different than Fort Dix, NJ.

We awoke to the sound of the drill sergeants' shouting and banging. If you tried to stay in bed they would throw you out of the bed, mattress and all. It did not matter if you were in the top bunk or what; they threw this one dude out of the top bunk. Once out of bed we got into groups and cleaned the barracks from top to bottom. At first you fixed your bunk with military corners and all, and then you joined the sweep crew, the mop crew or the floor shine crew. We usually did not have to wax the floor but it did need to be buffed everyday. You could look down the center aisle of the barracks and see the sunlight shining off of the floor.

We had such a diverse group of cultures. Everyday you heard music that at first sounded strange, it did not sound good at first but then it wore on you. Once you learned the words you were likely to sing them. I listened to all of the music from Bon Jovi to Parliament Funkadelics.

By a certain time we had to be outside and formation. Once in formation the "Top Sarge" the barracks would speak to us. I can't recall s name but he was a cool customer. I observed w he ran things. We would have role call, d receive our mail. We saluted the flag to the mpets sound of "Reverie" and ended the day th "Taps".

Then we broke off into our different MOS's. Most of us were either in supply, or cooks, like I was. Cooking classes were okay. I think I looked forward to the meals that we could eat once we were done. I still remember that first class of us standing around tables listening to all of the instructions about safety and food preparation that we were to partake in. There were about four stages of cook school.

One was in the kitchen where we prepared meatloaf, omelets, and a whole chicken amongst other things. Then we were moved to baking school where we were taught how to bake pastries from scratch, using yeast. I remember the instructor telling us to walk very quietly because we could damage the baked goods as they begin to rise in the oven. Baking was very fun to me.

Our other type of cook school was field cooking. This is where you are taught to prepare food out in the fields as if you were feeding infantry men who were on and off the battlefield. We learned how to set up, clean and take down the portable kitchen area.

The last part of cook school was working in the actual kitchen preparing breakfast, lunch and dinner. Let me tell you being a cook is one of the demanding MOS's in the military. We had to wake up and be at the kitchen by 4:30 a.m. then we would not leave until every thing was done, around noon.

I once prepared this big soup with a real large spoon and a bowl so big, that you would have thought I was preparing a witches brew. I needed help from one of the experienced sergeants who was a master cook. He worked on it with me until we had something that the troops would like. Some of the troops were saying that they liked the soup.

We were mainly runners, cleaners and servers for the real cooks. I used to like to stand on the mess line and fix the hamburgers. Those troops' would be so excited to get their burgers. They used to say I want a cheeseburger, yeah that one right there. They would hold over their plates in anticipation while I dropped the burgers onto their plates. Once we served them we could eat twice as much as they could because they had to go back to their MOS, but we were already at ours!

I met some good friends at this camp. We had a lot of fun. My man from Louisiana used to tell a lot of stories. We used to watch television in the TV room or shoot pool or something.

Somebody pulled out the boxing gloves one day. We were standing in the windows of the bays when somebody yelled that Private Green and Private Smith were boxing. I eagerly watched them because I had boxed many times before. I noticed carefully if I thought the two guys were good boxers or not. After a while we were all commenting how silly they both looked because neither one was doing much damage to the other.

One of the guys mentioned to Private Green that I had said that he could not box. So as I was walking down the bay the next day, my man from Louisiana started instigating a fight between Green and me. He told me that Green wanted to box me and I said come on. Then he said that Green wanted to fight me and that Green said he knew Karate. I said, no problem, tell Green that I know the "Marquis of Queensbury". Louisiana went back and told Green and came back to me and said "Green had asked, what is that"? I said, "tell him, don't worry about it, if he wants to fight me, he will find out". I didn't hear another peep out of Green again. [Marquis of Queensbury is just the rules of boxing that governed the sport in the early days, I was merely telling Green and Louisiana that I knew how to fight].

One day I almost got myself in a heap of trouble. A guy I briefly knew had about a quarter or so of "reefer". He was supposedly selling it on the base. I knew that took some nerve. We had just started hanging together when we were sitting in the staircase of the bays. He was rolling some joints and I remember people were asking him for some but he would tell them something like they had to pay for it.

He was sitting up a little higher than I was and before we knew it, there was Sarge looking down right over us. He said what you got there son? This particular Sarge was known by all of us to be a butt hole! He was not someone you wanted to rub shoulders with. He made me and the dude go with him to see "Top Sarge". He threatened us with strong actions. I remember him telling me that they would send me to Fort Leonardwood for five years, if I did not tell Top Sarge, that the dude was selling "reefer".

I knew that I could not squeal on my friend and did not plan to do so. But the implication of being with the guy and serving time in Leonardwood for something I was not involved in was not attractive. Once I got into "Top Sarge's" office he did not ask me anything that amounted to squealing on my friend. He just asked me if I was with him. I told him I was just sitting on the bay steps. Then I was dismissed.

I would catch the bus back home from Fort Lee on some weekends and ride back to DC. I think I did this to be with my girlfriend and family. The bus ride was about three hours from home. One time I was late (AWOL) so I had to call in that morning and let them know my whereabouts.

The first time that I got off the bus in DC with my military uniform on was very strange. I noticed the extra looks that I received from people. This made me very paranoid. I did not understand that they liked looking at a U.S. serviceman in uniform. It was so good to ride up in front of your building and jump out of that cab. The Army had begun to make a new man out of me.

18

OUR FAVORITE BROTHER

Having four brothers and being the middle brother, was a blessing. I had two to lead me, and two for me to take the lead on. The older two used to say "naw Harp you're different, we don't want you to do this or that, they did not want me to follow in their footsteps. They wanted me to go to college and be something because that is what they saw in me. Of all the times we lived together, they only took me up on the hill once to hang with them. That was right after I had left the Army. Eric was against it at first but Jay convinced him to let me hang one night up on the hill with them.

It was just like any other night though. We did the same things I did with my old buddies except the people were their friends. I felt out of place and soon I began, giving these kids some change, I was drunk and gave away a little too much money. That's when reality set in and I took my behind home feeling foolish but saying I had learned a lesson in it.

JT was truly the special one. He had to be special because he was the one that the Lord took home first. He just lived his life about five times faster than most of us did. We all called him Jay or JT for short. When JT was a young boy he busted his head wide open. He fell from a concrete porch and hit his head on concrete ground! He might have received stitches, it was a nasty gash. We kind of assumed that happened because he was trying to hit a bird with a rock, earlier that day. That meant bad luck if you hit or killed a bird, we used to say.

He grew up in an environment where he had to fight or get his butt kicked early. Having just one older brother and one older sister he knew that hanging with the bad guys was his best avenue to make it through. I guess he was naturally inclined to the fast lane anyways. It didn't take him very long to become one of the leaders.

I remember the time when the two twins rode their bikes to our house and jumped him because he had fought one of them at school. Rick and I were walking him to the dumpster and the twins were waiting for him on their bicycles. They approached him and one or both of them punched him in the face. Rick and I were afraid and we couldn't do much if we wanted too...all we did was throw rocks at them as the twins sped away on their bikes. That did not stop him even though he was crying from the ordeal. The next day he got a couple of guys and they went after the twins and fought them again. I was like a reporter the next day trying to get all of the information I could from him.

He used to always get reports from school that he was not going to class or fighting or something. He was not a disrespectful kid because our parents raised us right. They taught us to respect adults and don't put your hands on someone unless they raised their hands at you first. He was just a kid that stayed into trouble and mischief.

I was very anti drugs in those days, much of that mindset has been with me all of my life. I was very much into the anti-drug posters that the Washington Redskins put out. I looked up to athletes, and if they did not do drugs, then doing drugs had to be wrong! I aspired so much to become an NFL football player, and they were my role models.

Once he and my oldest brother took me up the hill to the basketball court and I noticed that they were smoking something. I kept asking them and they later told me they had smoked marijuana. I thought that my world had almost caved in! You see I was only about 11 at the time and they were around 14 and 15. Even though I was their little brother I was very smart and they knew it. I lectured and preached to them about the dangers of using drugs.

I wanted to see them make it because I knew I was going to try to do it right. I told them to go up to the police boys club to play sports. I tried to inspire my brother that he could make the football team as a quarterback. I told my other brother to not lose his love for baseball and to join the team at the boys club. They did not really listen. They just told me to not tell mama and diddy they were smoking drugs.

I found out that by the time Jay was in middle school he was skin popping. This caught me as a shock because the guy that told me was our friend Donny and I knew he would know. He did not have to lie on Jay like that because they were good friends. I did not want to believe it because we could never tell that he was high. You know that dopey drudgery look. I don't remember seeing him "nodding", like those on heroin often do.

Before all of this, he and I used to share the same bedroom. I used to always question him and he would tell me these interesting stories about the things he was doing like his fights, girls, his mischief, you name it. He loved to dance and act silly, so he was always goofing off.

He and I would sit for hours and play 500 Gin Rummy and do card tricks. He would deal sometimes three cards which made playing 500 more challenging. I on the other hand would deal around 15 cards which made the game more exciting because you could spread all over the place. He learned this card trick when he came back from the Job Corps in Indiana; he only stayed about four months because he got kicked out. He said that some guy had humped him when they were in line and he turned around and hit the guy.

Jay learned this card trick that was so funny and cool, he asked us. "Do ya'll want to see the Queen dance"? He said "I bet you I can make the Queen dance; do ya'll want to see the Queen dance"? He said, "OK, but ya'll have to chant and get her ready, and she will dance for ya, so he said keep chanting, "Dance, Queen dance! We started chanting, "dance Queen dance" he said "louder" and we were yelling, "dance Queen dance"! "dance Queen dance"!

Slowly with the deck of cards in his hand and the Queen at the top, he began to slowly push the Queen up so we could see her peeking up at us, as if she was bashful. He told us to chant louder. We had to chant, to encourage her to dance for us. As the Queen got halfway up, he takes the card and says, "Ah do, do, do" all the while wobbling the card around as if the Queen is dancing, but he's just moving the card around. We went "ahhhhhh, you tricked us", and he was laughing hard at how he fooled us.

He used to hit on us and pick on us until we had our mother get him to stop. He and my older brother would pick on me until I got red in the face. Once I became really angry, I would get so angry that I would fight them even if they hit me harder. I would almost black out and start swinging wildly at them. They used to yell out "he is getting red" and that meant I was about to get after them and they knew it. So they would try to calm me down then...all the while laughing. You know when you are laughing real hard and someone is trying to get you, but you are too weak to really fight back, that's how they would be. But by then, I was like a fire-breathing dragon!

Once I got so mad at my mother because she intervened when my sister Dorothy and I, were fighting. She slapped me and I balled up my fist at her. That only caused her to say "you bad enough to hit me, come on, I will knock you on that floor". I was still calculating my next move, until my brother Eric kept telling me to "get a grip, David you betta get a grip on yourself"! I had already gotten dealt with by Dorothy; she could fight as well as I could because she was bigger and stronger that I was. Since I could not beat her fighting, and really did not want to fight her anymore that day, I went into her room and knocked over the belongings on her dresser top. That was when mama jumped in on it. She hit me with an open hand and I was about to black out. I got two beatings that day, one from my sister and one from my mama!

Shortly after I had left Advanced Individual Training at Fort Lee, life began to really slow down. I had begun to accept the schedule of waiting till everybody woke up and sitting down to get high around 2 or 3 o'clock in the afternoon. I knew that I wanted a job, or a career but I was also settling into the laid back attitude, all the while not wanting to fail. I just was not able to find work and had no skills for anything. This particular morning I was gazing out the window like I always did, in the silence of the apartment. My brothers and sisters usually slept late; I was the first one to go to bed and the first one to wake up. Things were quite boring outside with the usual traffic and people going into the social services annex building just across the street.

Then I spotted this young lady walking down the street. The young lady stopped and stumbled like to the ground. She was moving about the ground as if she was waddling in the dirt. I could tell that something was wrong with her.

Was she high, was she lost and confused, was she retarded? What was the matter with her? I immediately ran for Jay, to get his take on it, and his advice.

Jay had only been out of jail, I would say for about a month, he was sleeping in the room with his girlfriend, Saundra. He actually had two girlfriends at the same time named Saundra. I said "Jay, come look at this girl outside, she is acting crazy!" He got up and looked out the front room window and then we said "let's go out there". I was quite concerned for her mental stability and circumstances, and I was also hoping that she was alright (not retarded) and able to hang with us. After all, we drank and smoked weed from noon to midnight!

Jay did something that I would never forget, as we walked over there I ran down all of the scenarios, hoping that he could rap (talk) to her and bring her inside, so she could cool down. When we got there, he asked her what her name was, and if she was ok? I don't think the young lady could answer him coherently but maybe she could. He asked her where did she live and did she need some help? JT then hailed down a taxi cab for the young lady, who was about his age, maybe just a little older, and put her inside the cab.

He reached in his pocket and paid the cab fare. Then he told the driver a little about the situation and asked the cab driver to take her home, where she said she lived. I found that truly remarkable! I really did! It left an even better feeling in me than if she had come back to the apartment with us! I remember him saying "if that had been his sister, he would have wanted someone to do the same thing for her".

What a lesson learned! I guess that is why to this day, I am so concerned to look out for the person that may be in harms way. When I see little kids walking too far alone by themselves, or a person really in need physically or mentally, I want to help that person, or I pray that they would make it safe to their destination.

He told me that the worse thing to do is to rape a woman or molest a child. He said that when a rapist, or child molester get sent to jail, they get the worst treatment from the prisoners. He said that the "residents of the prison" feel that it could have been someone in their family that it happened too and they couldn't do anything about it, because they were locked away. It could have been their child, mother, sister, or girlfriend and they will take no pity on any perpetrator that commits those crimes.

There was the other time when Jay and I were walking up the street heading to McGogney Elementary school. We saw these three guys walking down the sidewalk coming towards us. One of the dudes bumped into me and that set off a few nasty words. This guy was the same dude that had threatened us many years ago in a basement with a pistol. I recognized him and Jay knew who he was from the hill. He knew the type of guys they were, older than he, but more ruthless and experienced ex-offenders. The dude thought I was going to back down but I wanted to fight him. Jay however, told me to let it go because they probably had guns on them and they had an extra man too. After a few more angry words from the dude we all just backed away from each other. After being in the Army for five months I had a little edge to me. I was used to having to deal with guys all of the time.

When Jay and I used to walk up to McGogney playground where we hung out with the 10th street and Trenton Place dudes, I would often ask him questions to see where his mind was at. One day I asked him, "Why don't you just find a good little job, get married, settle down and have some kids. That seemed so easy and plain to me to do. Jay told me basically that "he couldn't because his mentality was in the fast lane." He was a hustler, that's all that he knew. He wanted to make his money by hustling. Early on it was robbery, then selling smoke.

One day after I had worked my summer job, the one at Crispus Attucks Recreation where we were alley cleaners, Jay and his friend Reggie drove me uptown to pickup my check. I was only expecting a hundred dollars or so, and I had promised to give them ride fare and a little extra for "git high". I picked up that check and I saw that they had actually given me over three hundred dollars for retroactive payments. I was so happy, almost in shock. I showed it to Jay and he said, "Dave, you are a lifesaver". I gave him $100.00 so he could pick up a pound of reefer and hustle it. It kept him on his feet for awhile. Eric was angry that I had given it to Jay and not to him first, he would have actually turned it over better than Jay would, he said.

Jay would take his girlfriends little daughter on walks with us up the street to the McGogney playground. This is where he used to reflect, and see his life clearer. Just before he died, he took my brother Vest up there. He gave him his watch, told him he wanted him to have it. He told him that this is where he goes when he has problems that he needed to think through.

McGogney sits on a hill, a long street called Wheeler Road. You could stand on McGogney's field or parking lot and see a panoramic view of the area. You could see, Oxon Run Creek, which we always called "the creek". You could see the Valley Green apartments, which we called "the Valley" or "Valley Green". To the right you could see the large "Hi-Rise" apartment. You could also see "Condon Terrace", Hart Jr. High school, and other apartments. Looking at the scenery from McGogney was very peaceful and mind settling because you were looking down into a "valley". It was a concrete valley, of misery, hope, despair, and fun memories also.

If you spent anytime in the "valley" you came out a different person. The "Valley" was not the most hospitable place to "outsiders". We used to call everybody that was not from the valley or southeast for that matter, a "bama"! That was Jay's favorite word. He used that word regularly, way, before everyone else was using it around there. He would say, the "bama" this or the "bama tried to chump us", or "look at that bama, you can tell he is not from around here, by the way that he is dressed". Later on he changed his word to "cad" as in "that cad ass nigga (dude)".

Somewhere in my life they started calling me "Harp". I am sure Jay had a lot to do with that. That is what he used to call me first it seems. Somehow I went from "Dave" to "Harp". That was an honor, to be the one to have the last name, as a nickname.

Jay was tall and rangy for his age. He was a good athlete, not very fast but fast enough. He could almost beat Donnie running and Donnie was fast! Jay had a good arm for a quarterback and was tough. I remember he was the quarterback for our sprawling football team. We had heard about this team and joined it with our friend Ricky. We were the Assumption Church team, a rag tag group of boys who most had never played organized contact football and coaches that did not know much about forming a tackle football team from scratch. I was the youngest and smallest boy in the whole league! I probably weighed 62lbs with rocks in my pocket! I had no business out there. I was there because my brother was playing, and I loved football as much as he did!

When we played the Wayne Place Chiefs we would get crushed. They beat us that first game 32-0! He took a beating too. Our line could not block for him and he would be scrambling around back there about to evade or break one tackler, but there would always be another guy to hit him. Crack, Crack! I used to hate seeing him take that pounding.

The Wayne Place Chiefs were very intimidating, organized, and good! I remember when they came to the field they had on these red uniforms just like the Kansas City Chiefs in the NFL wore and they ran a lap around the field in single formation. They had almost twice as many boys as we had and they had played ball in other football leagues. I did not play in that game or much of the others either. I only remember playing in one play on the kick return team the entire season. I ran to this big dude and threw a roll at his ankles. He jumped right over me and kept running to the ball carrier. I slowed him down because he did not make the tackle. I took all of my beatings in practice, playing offensive or defensive line, but it made me tougher though.

Jay also had a chance to go to New York and compete in a track meet as a long jumper but he did not go. I believe that he barely missed the cut. It would have been a good experience for him because Donnie's track speed had started to take him places.

Jay was the comical brother. He was the one playing the practical jokes, not really practical jokes, but things to kind of aggravate you. He wasn't always the life of the room, sometimes quiet, but still engaging. He commanded attention by his presence. Tall, dark, and handsome with a smooth assuring mannerism, a confident walk that caught many a women's eye. He could dance his head off. He was very smooth and cool when he hand danced. He and my older siblings used to dance "the Bop" together. Pairing up, they would hand dance with the male guiding the female in turns or coordinated steps. I could never quite dance the way they could.

In his late teens he got a youth act charge for armed robbery. He stuck up a grocery store, and was sentenced to two years in the Lorton Youth Center. Visiting him at times was something that you were melancholy about having to do. It left you feeling sad knowing that he had to stay behind while you were going back home. Sometimes seeing him standing there at the fence seeing you off while you were going to the parking lot, was hard to get over.

Jay played quarterback for the Lorton Youth Center teams. He used to tell me that he never had much of a line and that they usually got beat by the other teams. I used to get him to tell me about his experiences at the youth center all of the time. I looked up to him so I was always quizzing him about his experiences. As we got older I often gave him advice and mentored him to get away from the street life. He was a hustler for sure. He told me that was all that he knew. I would ask him if he hurt anybody and he would tell me if he did or not. I don't remember him saying he hurt anyone violently unless they tried to get him. He knew better because we were raised right, despite the road that he chose to live.

He was taken away from the family, way too early, figuratively by being incarcerated repeatedly, since the age of 18. But you could always count on Jay in some respect. Even now I count on him since he died because he helped make me who I am today. He taught me how to be tough. He taught us all how to be tough. That is why he used to hit on his little brothers, to make them ready for this world. Sometimes he would hit us soft; sometimes he would hit us hard and then really hard. He would hit us until we fought him back. He would often beckon to us to stop whining. Stop crying, stand up and be a man.

He once took a criminal charge for our younger

brother Vest and did time for it, because he, not Vest, was already on probation. Vest had been seen under surveillance selling pot with a certain jacket on. Fearing that Vest would be caught sooner or later if he was seen again with that jacket in the vicinity, he switched coats with Vest and went back to the same spot. Being that they were somewhat similar in physical appearance although Jay was considerably taller than Vest, he was arrested and charged. He said he did not want his little brother to go to jail at a young age, fearing that he wasn't ready for it, at the time.

I just wish that they would have burned the coat and stayed away from that hill for awhile. The "hill" is what we called the top middle of our housing projects, also the place where weed, dust and coke was sold openly in the streets. I remember this episode like it was yesterday. It was a cold, cold day. Snow was on the ground and Vest had been wearing his very distinctive jacket. The one that was a shiny silver jacket, it looked like a coat made of aluminum foil. This jacket was warmer than any coat; it had dark blue fur inside of it. We used to tease Vest about that coat. Few boys in all of DC had a jacket like it at the time.

Jay was in and out of prison since his first incarceration. Just when you got used to him being around for a while he was back in prison. He went from Virginia, to the District of Columbia, to New York, DC again and back to Virginia.

I could count on him the day that we had the trouble at the Eastover Shopping Center. On this particular day, my mother had taken Vest, Mark and myself to Sears and Roebucks off of

Alabama Ave. I bought a pair of jeans with my summer job money and a bicycle cable for my ten speed bike. I cherished that ten speed bike. It had to be one of the best gifts that I ever had. Not finding all of the clothes she had set out to find for my brothers we went over to Eastover Shopping Center in Oxon Hill, Md. Oxon Hill is just outside of southeast DC. It is only about three miles straight down Valley Avenue where we grew up.

While we were in JC Penny my brother had sat down my bag and it was stolen. I was so heartbroken. I paced frantically around the store hoping to find it. Mom let Vest and I walk down the concourse to see if we could spot the bag.

When I got down the concourse, I spotted this group of guys hanging out. I could tell they were young hoodlums and braced myself for trouble. I knew from my days at Johnson that if nothing else they were going to say something to us. One of the guys approached me for some money...I told him that I did not have any money. Then he put his hands on my pockets as if to check me for change. He was about my age and I was not scared of him. I was already in a rage because I had lost my shopping bag. Once he patted my pocket, I just hauled off and stole him in the mouth! I hit him so hard that his tooth cut a gash on my knuckle. That's when all of his boys jumped up in excitement.

Seeing that we were out numbered and also facing older boys, I told Vest to take off running. We met our mother and told her about the incident. She quickly gathered us in the GC Murphy store and made a phone call home. It seemed like no more than 15 minutes when my brother Jay and Diddy were walking swiftly down the concourse. We had to go back by the boys because that was on the way out...and besides the older boys were by then threatening us to come out of the store. We walked down the concourse kind of inconspicuous that we had two experienced helpers. As soon as we approached them the boys stood, ready to get us and, Wham!

My father and Jay started whopping their asses! I heard one guy saying, "c'mon JT, I did not do nothing to your brother". I could hear JT saying, "you messing with my brother?" All the while whipping the dude like he had stolen something from us. Diddy, had this dude against the wall throwing left and right hooks and haymakers, just like something you would see on television.

Of course some of those guys had known my brother because back then he and his friends would go everywhere shooting dice, going to parties and fighting. I don't know of too many times that Jay would not get into a fight at a party or a dance club. So these guys knew of him because they hung in some of the same circles. Even though they lived over in another complex, west of where we lived.

After Jay and my father got tired of kicking those butts, they let me and the dude finish our fight, right in the parking lot of the shopping center. I wanted to finish the fight too because the dude thought he was all bad. I hated dudes that thought they were so bad and caused trouble for everyone. I could have taken care of the dude like a bad cold. I even began to hold back because I felt that if they caught up with me again I had to save something. I could not show him everything. I also begin to hold back because it felt weird fighting in front of my parents. They said that I beat the fight although I didn't feel that I did too much.

Sure enough I ran into the dude again at the high school, two months later. And guess what? Jay was already locked up again in jail! I was out numbered again because the dude was with a group of dudes shooting dice on the side of the school building. Gary and I were walking around the school when I heard them spot me.

Someone went "hey, ain't that the dude we was fighting down Eastover?" So the guy I was fighting rose up and said something to me. I was a little scared considering the circumstances. But they did not know that Jay was back in prison, like I knew he was. Plus I was determined to fight the guy no matter if all of his boys were around. I also felt that I might have had some allies there because I knew somebody knew who my brother was...somebody in that crap game was from Johnson or the Valley and they knew who I was. If nothing else the dudes who we fought down Eastover knew who JT was.

He started talking crap to me, and I started mouthing back. All the while I could hear Gary saying, "C'mon Dave don't say nothing. It's too many of them." I'm like, "naw, naw, I am tired of him, I got to finish it once and for all!" He asked me if I had wanted to fight him, I said "c'mon down here...I ain't scared of you!" I knew in my heart that I was not going to hold back that time.

I was going to put on a boxing lesson that he would remember for a long time! But somehow maybe they thought about JT and dad, and the lesson that they learned at Eastover, so we did not fight again. We left the scene with my dignity still intact...but I was a little nervous. I usually did not let nervous energy stop me from fighting. As we where leaving, I told Gary the story of what had happened to us down at Eastover.

I was not one to act bad, walk around with a chip on my shoulder or anything. I was quite the opposite, even though I had two big brothers to back me up. I was old enough to know that just about everybody had big brothers or cousins to back them up too. Plus I knew that my brothers had their hands full also. There were lots of bad dudes in the Valley some badder than they ever were. Many guys had reputations that preceded them; some were already heading to "folklore".

We always thought of ourselves, my siblings, as having no back up except, Momma and Diddy. So Diddy always taught us to stick together. Mom and dad did not have brothers and sisters, so our Aunts and uncles were great aunts and uncles, older people. That was not really the case, because mama had half brothers and sisters that lived only about 4 miles away. The boys turned out to be some of the roughest dudes on that side of town. They had a reputation that we only wished that we had back then...but we rarely kept in contact with them.

This is why JT became the person that he was, because he did not have anyone to fight for him that he could run to on a regular basis, he had to rely on his friends. You know dads had to work and they were not running around fighting for their kids. My father sometimes worked two jobs. I would hear him leave in the morning and see him coming through the door in the mid evening, sometimes, only seeing him eat his dinner before my bedtime.

I was just the opposite of JT in many ways. I was sort of like his alter ego, his good angle, always telling him, "Jay you know that's not right, why did you do that" or "I hope you don't hurt anybody" or something of a concerning nature.

The last time I saw JT alive was one evening, after I had married and was living away from home, me and two of my buddies went on a "reefer run". It had to be "God's will" and "His" perfect timing because we ended up going down Wheeler Road from the top of Alabama Avenue. Just as we were turning off of Alabama Avenue, I saw this dude trying to hail a cab with his hand raised in the air. The cab driver just ignored him and I started laughing at that.

Unbeknownst to me it was JT, my brother! He crossed the street in front of us and I recognized him from the back seat. I said "Jim, that's my brother, hold up, that's my brother. I didn't think to ask Jim to give him a ride, but I stuck my head out of the window and said, "Jayyyy, it's me "Harp". He looked at me and said "hey Harp"! I was thinking where are you going? He waved his arms in the air and said "I'm gone Harp". "I'm gone". About a week later he was dead. He died of an apparent overdose of heroin.

One person that was with him in his last days accounted for the fact that he was tired and ready to leave this miserable world. Bill told us that Jay kept talking about payday. He could not wait until payday. Jay was in a half-way house at the time and had found employment. When Friday came said he was going to get paid.

While in the half-way house an informant (one of his girlfriends) called a tip hotline and told a lie to the detectives, that he was the perpetrator of a crime that he did not commit. She did this to get back at him for having another woman. She admitted to Jay and my brother Eric while they were sitting around getting high one evening. Jay said later to Eric, "did you hear what that b**** just said"? "She was laughing about lying on me and snitching to the police".

I had known that he was in jail at the time of the specific crime. He had just visited me at our new apartment shortly after he got out, and some of the crimes had already taken place because I had seen them on the news earlier in the year.

With that information he became the prime target. The detectives were relentless in their pursuit of finding all of the clues they could, to pin the crime on him. They showed up one day and harassed my sister in my mom's apartment, barging in the door with attitudes, claiming clothing that my sister could not identify as belonging to my brother. She knew what kinds of clothes that he wore because we all wore each others clothes. They tried to say they had certain clothes that none of us had before. He said things like, "I know he did it, and we are going to nail him!"

Jay had passed the line up, and they still were not satisfied that they had the wrong man.

So they had him slated to take a lie detector test after that. This is what he would find out the day that I last saw him, shortly after he got back to the half-way house.

Jay began to lose himself a little before this time. One day he smoked some PCP and he went into a hallucinogenic fit, taking off his clothes, running around outside, trying to hit or cut himself. This was not the same brother who had comforted me when no one else knew I was hurting.

Jay was fresh out of jail and he walked into the Southview Gardens' apartment that my mom had. I was so glad to see him because missing him had taken its toll on me. At that time I was also depressed because I felt that I was wasting away my life. I had just gotten out of the Army, living at home with momma, my sister, and two younger brothers was no fun at all. Momma was hard on us at that time, it seemed like me and Mark took most of the flack because we were always home. Every time she came home from work she would be yelling, about the house not cleaned up, or me sitting around not working, and Mark not going to school and laying up in his bed all day long.

After Dorothy would pack up her son, and go off to daycare and work, the empty apartment would become my enemy. I had no one to really talk to, no one to care. No job. No money. No friends. I contemplated slitting my wrist, or other forms of suicide that would not hurt me as I went out. Lying on that sofa that day, I was in shear misery. You know the kind where you shake, cry, mumble, and talk to yourself. Hoping the phone would ring so you could talk to someone.

Then Jay walked through the door. He knew that something was not right with me so he began to talk to me. He told me about how he had to go "cold turkey" and kick his heroin addiction in a jail in White Plains, NY. I found him preaching to me about things were going to be alright, trust in the Lord, he would make it better. I had told him that at times I wanted to commit suicide...he gave me the courage to go on.

Sometime later I enrolled in the "Smith Business School" and my career finally got off the ground. It was in this school that I saw Jay display another act of strength. Me and a couple of my girlfriends from school used to sit in McPherson Square and light up a joint. There was this musical festival going on that day and we were out having a good ole time. I looked up, and coming through the crowd was Jay, with his confident gait and long stride. I said "hey there is my brother, I had to show off my brother to the girls, you know. I was like "Jay c'mon you are just in time, let's get high, we was about to smoke some herb". "What you doing way up here, where you going man?" Jay said "naw Harp, I can't. I am about to see my parole officer and take a piss test". I was like "ahhhh, okay man, I understand." But boy was I glad that my classmates had seen my brother.

After I got out of the Army and got back home, things began to really slow down. It seemed like I had no reason for existence. We had moved from my old neighborhood to Southview Apartments and I had to find new friends. I didn't know what to do. I didn't have any real skills or experience, and no one to give me a job or help me find a job. My family had expected so much out of me and I was beginning to let them down. Nothing was on the television and I could not stand the soap operas. The only one I really started watching was "General Hospital" but it came on so late in the day.

One day I started going into this long tantrum about life, mainly missing JT, who was always "locked up". I starting complaining, feeling sorry, talking out loud, rambling, so anyone could hear me while I was standing in the window. This was the same guy that I almost took a knife for when we were in a gang fight that started between him and his girlfriend. I had just come out of the Army and when the fights were over this girl was walking towards me. She kind of had a smile on her face and I really didn't think anything of her, but she had a butcher knife in her hand behind her back. If it wasn't for this dude that knew her, he grabbed her and asked her what she was doing with that knife; I might have gotten cut.

Another time, I walked in the snow back to my old neighborhood, I was on a pity mission, something compelled me to walk, and I ended up back in that same apartment that we had grew up in. It was abandoned by then and I noticed all of the dirty syringes, reefer roaches and trash that littered the apartment. But it did something to soothe my spirit because I realized that I wasn't leaving anything that I needed back there. Except for the pictures that I had left on the wall, I felt better when I started back home. I only wished that I had taken photos of the walls with my pictures on them.

Let me digress, there was the time when my brothers and their friends were shooting up in the next room and one of the guys began overdosing. I heard panic and fear coming from the room, one of my brothers was giving orders to go get some ice to put under the guys testicles, to hold the guy up, keep smacking him, make him walk, whatever it took to keep him conscious. They prevailed because the ambulance never came for the guy, they kept him alive!

Jay needed more than himself, to save himself, from this "dark world". He was ready to go and see "Jesus". He told Bill "when payday comes, let's shoot up". "Those detectives are trying to get me for something I did not do", I am gonna handle it, when "payday" comes".

Bill told him that he wasn't up to it, so he found "Cha Cha" that day. Rumor has it that he and "Cha Cha" bought some heroin, probably some "brown Mex" that was super potent. It is no doubt that Jay plunged that needle into his arm. Not wanting to release the plunger and pull out the syringe. He had probably already told Cha Cha that this was his last time. "Take the money out of my pants, because I won't need it anymore". This was the kind of man that he was, considerate to the very end, although his life often seemed to dictate otherwise.

He was definitely a "lady's man" the girls were crazy about him, just ask Towanda, Janice, Phyllis, Jo Anne, Saundra, Sandra, Vicki, and a few others whom I do not know or remember.

At his wake, a friend and former inmate with him told my mother that, "JT said he was never coming back to prison again, he was tired of it"! "He said he and JT used to have to fight sometimes standing back to back, with weapons, while being outnumbered. JT had his back many times...but he said he was through with the prison life once he got out."

Jay was buried on my 23rd birthday! I remember it as being the saddest day of my life! I could not even think about my birthday. All we did as a family was cry and moan. We sat around that table and cried. All it took was for one of us to start crying and that would start everyone else to cry. I remember mama saying, "He was my Rock of Gibraltar", she said, "A parent is not supposed to bury their children"!

Back then, what we did on most Friday and Saturday nights was sit around the house and be a family. We drank, some smoked cigarettes, we smoked outside, we listened to music and raised the children in our new roles of parenthood. Most every weekend night we gathered at momma's apartment to do this.

When we started the repast, Vicki, his closest girlfriend at the time, started crying out loud. She said, "Jay, where are you going?" She said that "JT had just walked out of the bedroom past us, and said he was going up on the hill". None of us tried to doubt what she had just seen because you never know about that kind of stuff.

Later on that night, we were all sitting around the table, only the immediate family was left, the usual weekend crew. We were crying, and finally, I had a "eureka" thought! I was like we have to find a way to stop crying...maybe think about something else. In an instant, I said, "hey ya'll, today is still my birthday!" Momma said, "Yeah, you're right!" "Let's celebrate it"! So we all started making plans to go to the liquor store and to Popeye's before they closed. We all hopped into my brother-in-law Jonathan's car and rode to the stores.

When we got back, there was no more crying collectively, we all began to heal together as a family. It took me a solid year before I did not mourn for him everyday. Once I realized that he was with me in my memories, I began to celebrate the 23 years that I knew him. I'm sure it took some of us much longer to heal.

Several years later, my sister was going through some of my brothers belongings and she stumbled across a bible that he had owned while in prison. In it were the words that on a certain day, he had committed his life to the Lord! That is where those words of faith and consolation had come from to console me earlier in my depression.

19

GOD SPEAKS

I came to know the Lord as my savior February 7, 1988. It was my wife's (at the time) birthday; she had cooked a nice breakfast and asked me to go to church with her. I usually did not want any part of her church but I felt compelled to pay my first visit there. A month or so later, I was in my room, all alone in the house. It was a sunny Saturday afternoon, everyone was out doing chores and I decided to go into my room to pray. I was probably reading the bible at the time and felt an "unction", or "calling" to pray. Before long, I was praying about Jay, who had passed away about four years before.

I was trying to plead his case and ask God to admit him into heaven. I really was! I was being his advocate. I was actually asking God to accept my brother into heaven! You know God actually knows our hearts and he knows everything anyways so I could not tell him anything about

Jay that he already did not know. (This was before my sister had found that bible).

I was "putting on the dog" too, praying fervently! Crying, snotting, begging, speaking in tongue, determined to stay down there until I heard from God. I was praying for quite some time, over 30 minutes at least, when God spoke to me. I heard his voice audibly, plainly, and distinctively, this time!

I knew exactly what he said. It went something like this, "God please accept Jay, please God, he really had a good heart, please accept him into heaven. I went on and on...God spoke and said, "CRUCIFY YOURSELF"! He did not holler, it was a calm voice. Let me tell you, it was as if he was right next to my ear. I paused to peak and see if anyone was there!

I was baffled and elated all at the same time! I kind of went "huh, what"? Then I caught myself questioning God, and I began to say "okay, okay, you are God", "whatever you say goes"! For a moment it was like, I had walked into the oval office of the United States and the President gave me an answer...but that is way too small of an analogy. The "oval office" should not even be mentioned in the same breath as the "throne room of God", the "Holy of Holies". That was only a mere earthly comparison that I could make at the time.

But just imagine hearing the "voice" of God spoken to you, while you are still alive on Earth. It is truly awesome! One other time I was walking alone and I thought I heard a voice say, "go to church"! It happened so fast that I wasn't sure if it had happened. (But I went to church that

Sunday!) This however was nothing like that. It was as clear as it was concise. God doesn't mix words. He says what he has to say and it is final!

Confused, I thought about it for weeks and then I understood later what God meant; what He was telling me. "Crucify yourself" meant for me to: 1) take care and or be concerned about my salvation, 2) it meant for me to get the "junk" or "ways" out of myself that hindered my relationship with God, and 3) to live for God foremost!

It took awhile for me to understand what it meant, but I caught on when Elder Danny Cook from my church, told me that he had to "crucify himself" whenever he went out to play basketball. Basically he had to get rid of the "old angry man", "the old flesh" the "old attitude" he had before he "became saved". He would prepare himself before he played basketball, thru prayer and meditation.

Rev. E.V. Hill once said in one of my favorite sermons, he preached at his beloved wife's funeral. He went on to tell the congregation how wonderful his wife was, *she truly was everything a man could want from a helpmate*! When God took her away from him, being a Pastor, he began to question God. With angry words of pain he began to attack God with questions. Why me, how could you take away my wife? Finally, God told him to "TRUST ME". That's all. God said "Trust me". All you can hear at the end of this message is Rev. Hill shouting "TRUST ME"! TRUST ME"! You've got to hear it; it will bring tears to your eyes.

I did not need to hear from God to believe in God anymore than I already had. I had faith, that God is real. But this nonetheless is one of those miracles that I can draw from when I hear arguments to the contrary. Nobody can take that away from me, "yes, God speaks!"

20

WHY I WROTE THIS BOOK

I am writing my story for several reasons. One of my main reasons is to help younger readers overcome some of the same obstacles that I faced in my early life. I feel that by sharing my struggles it can help someone who may go through the same thing.

Being the kind of person that I am, I really want to help people. Whether it is a kind word, a smile, advice, conversation, friendship, loyalty, whatever. I feel that we all would be better off if we "loved our fellow man"! The Bible says, "LOVE never fails, and to LOVE thy neighbor as thyself." *Can't we all just get along?*

My story is not some story where all sorts of tragedies occurred (thank God). It is not one of a central character that eventually has done something astonishing in the course of his or her life. It's a book by a normal character, who wants to share some of the events that have shaped his life. We all have a book to write about our life.

Many people have just as many interesting things that have happened to them over the course of their lifetime, and we can learn a lot from those various experiences. I hope that I didn't miss many of the real significant points about my life journey, as I conveyed them in this book.

Some of the stories I have shared are humorous, and that is the main reason why I put it in the book. All the while, I want to convey a message of certain experiences and thought processes in certain situations. Many of my stories were about sports. It has been my love for sports that I attribute my desire to read, to learn. By liking sports, I began to read more and more. I followed my dad's advice to read the sports pages every day, if nothing else. Some of my favorite books were Durango Street, Run Nigger Run, The Autobiography of Malcom X, and The Sensuous Man. The more I began to read, the more I became interested and knowledgeable to the world we live in.

This story is from the eyes of a young boy who grew up wanting the world to be a better place. I remember when we were kids over 25 years ago, my friend Flip and myself were having a philosophical conversation about life, growing up in the "projects," almost poor, and how we would write a book about what we felt then, or what we could do to turn things around. This is a part of that endeavor.

This entire book is from memory. Some of my insight may be a little distorted; however, none of it was done with any intention to change the course of how my life has unfolded, thus far.

Ironically, there was a television story made in the late 60's or early 70's called, "JT". It was about a young black boy growing up in the ghetto. I watched that story intensively, because it seemed like the story was made about our brother but it was slightly ahead of him. It had some parallels, which would make a great, modern day, true sequel, which can be this story.

A part of my writing this book is to relate to the children who are growing up in projects; the inner cities and suburbs, all over America, to get something positive out of every day occurrences. People usually comment that I always try to get something good out of everything. When you grow up in the "inner city", you learn how to adapt to a lot of things. You have to learn how to adapt to your environment or you won't survive.

Once again, I give all of the credit in the world to my parents, even my grandmothers, for although they were average people, they gave us the most important thing you can give another person, and that is Love! Without love, we would have never made it thus far. *For they who do not have much, have more than enough, with LOVE.* The bible says, that **"love covers a multitude of sins. For God so loved the world that he gave his only begotten son." Prayer is a part of that love**!

None of my experiences are written here to corrupt anyone. I turned out okay, but I wish that I had not found those stumbling blocks, that curtailed my aspirations. I do not advocate drinking, smoking, using drugs, and sex before marriage. **Boys and girls save yourself for that**

special day when you become married! I was young and should not have been doing those bad things myself.

However, I wanted to write about all of my experiences the way that they were and hopefully not glamorize anything that was bad. My intent is to dissuade the young reader from thinking, it is cool to use drugs, act "hard", or look "thuggish", selling drugs or following wrong the crowd.

That is something that I never wanted to do. I always wanted my individuality and followed my own drummer. Today many young people are carbon copies of the next person. I tried to dissuade my friends from doing things that we were not supposed to do. They labeled me with a nickname, they called me "Chicken" but looking back, I'm glad I earned that nickname. I did not want to end up in reform school or prison somewhere.

Personally I have experienced being teased, a broken home, drug and alcohol abuse, violence, prejudice, and low self-esteem as a child. I hope to help you gain confidence, strength, and inner-peace to make it thru tough times. Always know that you are special and God loves you!

Not too many people know how to be a "real person" a "real friend", a "class act", in this "dog-eat-dog mentality" that pervades the world today!

Children, be yourself, don't try to be like the next boy or girl, unless it is something positive! If your best friend makes the honor roll, then try to make it too! If your friend is a good athlete, then you try to become a better one! Don't play that thug roll, to fit in with the wrong crowd...*and for God sakes don't let anyone dissuade you and lose your dreams!!!*

I have always carried myself in ways that was different than the environment in which I grew up in. Most of my closest friends did the same, we aspired to go to college and make something of ourselves. I didn't act like I was from the ghetto. That was nothing to wear on your shoulder! That is nothing to really brag about. You might come from the ghetto, but you don't have to have the ghetto in YOU!

As for me, I made it off of those mean streets, I turned out okay. I've been to many years of college. I could have been a PHD by now, if I had stayed on one chosen academic path. I am an engineer by trade with a major telecommunications firm. I also volunteer with a good group of guys, at the high school level, where we coach football, the greatest sport ever invented!

But it was thru God, help from my family and my choices that enabled me to succeed in life!

Ask God today, to come into your life, tell him that you believe that Jesus Christ died for your sins, ask him to forgive you of your sins and choose to walk with him all the days of your life, for this is the **greatest gift of all**!

21

CONCLUSION

Our parents did the best they could to raise us. They gave us discipline, they taught us respect, they instilled in us to get an education. They may not have had a lot to give, but the most important thing was, they gave us love! That is what our children need. They need someone to care, to be there for them, to protect them, to discipline them.

Now I appreciate it that my dad made us stay in the house for weeks at a time. He made us read books and not run outside everyday. They also gave us a sense of unity! Family unity....to love your siblings and parents because someday we'll all need each other.

Violence is prevalent today. Just look at the gang wars in South Central, California, New York, DC and other cities across America. Look at the problems that my alma mater, Ballou Sr. High, has faced in the last few years. Look at how drugs have destroyed families and communities.

Back in the day, we fought with our hands; we did not resort to guns. Yeah, some of us were teased, picked on, victimized, you name it, but rarely was it settled with a bullet.

We have to stop killing one another, people! Wake up! Senseless violence is everywhere! People are becoming more, and more terrified.

God says in the bible to, "**fear not man, who can only kill the body; but fear God, who can not only kill the body, but damn the soul to hell**! (paraphrased Matthew 10:28)

Good night and God bless!

Thug

A little word that has too much say,
    About the mentality of our youth today
There is no love in this word,
    Void of a nice warm hug...

A word so strong it crosses genders,
    It's no wonder why our youth are so
hindered!
This word produces a mentality that
    Can lead to fatalities
If we don't change things

Who will take the blame for
    Not bucking this trend?
Parents, Family, or friends?

Will I take the blame,
    Will you take the blame?
Maybe our efforts will rid our shame!

David Harper

Printed in the United States
by Baker & Taylor Publisher Services